F
K83   Kolpacoff, Victor.
            The raid.

DATE	ISSUED TO

F
K83   Kolpacoff, Victor.
            The raid.

Temple Israel Library
2324 Emerson Avenue South
Minneapolis, MN. 55405

Please sign your name and telephone number
on the above card.

Books and materials are loaned for a period of
three weeks and may be returned to the Library
or Temple reception desk.

Fines will be charged for any damage or loss of
materials.

DEMCO

Books by Victor Kolpacoff

THE RAID
1971
PRISONERS OF QUAI DONG
1968

THE RAID

Victor Kolpacoff

THE RAID

Atheneum
New York 1971

This book is for Elaine,
who also suffered on the mountain

At the level of individuals, violence is a cleansing force. It frees the native from his inferiority complex and from his despair and inaction; it makes him fearless and restores his self-respect.

FRANTZ FANON
The Wretched of the Earth

THE RAID

Waiting

IN the glaring white light of an August noon, on the sun-baked ground, the three bodies lay with a terrible reality under their olive-green shrouds, only their faces and toes protruding under the canvas like the draped carvings atop a sarcophagus. What shocked was not that they were men, or that they had recently been men, but that they could now look so inhuman, that their nervous systems, the miraculous bone marrow and shining guts and thought could all be brought to this. The hard earth, the pebbles, and brittle shoots of desert grass under them were more living than these half human forms under green tarpaulins. One wondered how they had died, not just whether by bullet or shrapnel or splash of napalm and jellied gasoline, but about the quality of their deaths, whether they had died bravely or cowardly, suddenly, without the obligation of thought, or slowly and with recognition. Yet it was the manner of their deaths, Faisal reflected, looking down at them where he stood, half trembling, at the center of the barren camp, that was unthinkable. No matter how it came, those seconds or minutes it had taken each of them to die (When? For what reasons? Because of what mistakes?), those final seconds —surely one could not measure them by the ordinary standards of time. He wondered if the process of escaping their violated flesh had not, for these three, seemed like whole hours and days. For between the bullet that hit you and the death it brought did you not live another life, a second birth and death, stricken with that pain, whimpering or cursing, trying to fight back like an animal with the blade already in its heart?

Faisal wondered. Abruptly, then, he pulled the visor of his fatigue cap down tighter over his eyes, hoping by this movement of his hands, so full of life, so different from these three, to drive such thoughts away. Only moments ago the remnants of the patrol—one regular Jordanian army officer, a physician from Tripoli who was now a demolition expert, and three Palestinian refugees from Gaza—had come in with their dead. Or at least most of their dead. The truck from the Golan camp had met them where they had been instructed to wait inside the border at Ba'qleen. Faisal had watched the grim-faced, weary, mud-covered men walk to their tents to wash themselves, eat a mouthful of cold food, perhaps to sleep mindlessly through the heat of midday, to wake with a start at twilight knowing only that somehow they had survived.

He had overheard Ali explaining to Major Kassim, the camp's political officer.

"They say they were caught in the river by a helicopter. Abdullah, the leader of the patrol, had a heavy machine gun, but no antiaircraft sights. So, of course—"

Yet the Major had insisted that it was a good raid. A pumping station at Kibbutz Sha'al had been blown up, flooding the fields before they could be harvested. At least two Israeli militiamen were known dead, perhaps three. Of the five Fatahs killed, four were lost in the helicopter attack, against which they had no defense. There was no disgrace in that. It had been a good raid.

Nor was Faisal shocked because these three bodies lying under green canvas were the first guerrilla dead that he had seen, for he was already acquainted with the manner, the fear and suddenness, of night commando raids. They began with days of tedious planning, followed by the tense hours of infiltrating through darkness across the river, into the farms and across the patroled roads of the occupied territory, and ended, usually before sunrise, with a sudden, sharp exchange of fire with an enemy rarely seen, hardly real. After this came the desperate business of getting out before daylight exposed you in that barren hill country, the most inhospitable terrain on earth to guerrillas, where the enemy helicopters dropped down out of a blazing white sky, the sun always at their backs, like all the vengeful matrons of Israel screaming for their lost children. Once the guerrilla band had struck, every advantage lay with the enemy. This patrol had been caught that way. Perhaps they had been too slow; perhaps they were carrying wounded; perhaps they became lost; maybe it had been no one's fault, and they had done everything right, but the Jews had done better, a pilot, by purest chance, spotting them as helpless as dun-colored ants moving slowly against the gray rocky slopes of the Hebron Valley. Faisal himself had taken shrapnel in his leg on such a raid two months before. Numbed in the first shock, he had given himself up for lost, and told his comrades to go on without him. But when they left he found that he could walk perfectly well, despite the pain, and half an hour later he caught up with them, limping into a gulley where they had stopped to rest, feeling absurd for his display of sentimental heroism—"No, don't wait for me. Go on! Save yourselves!" He had been perhaps a trifle shocked, too, to find that his comrades could so willingly abandon him, but the sight of such deaths was common with them, it was expected. If they gave little comfort, they asked none for themselves. They ignored the danger to their lives as best they could, as one ignores fatalities of nature, earthquakes, and plagues, which seem merely problematical. Had they allowed themselves to reflect on their chances of surviving even one such raid they would never have mustered the courage to go out again. They had vowed to fight to liberate the homeland, and mostly they were grown men, not boys; therefore they knew that they had volunteered to die. The struggle would last a generation. Who could hope to survive so long? No, you fought to lay the groundwork on which others might, perhaps, march to final victory. The only question was when, in what manner, because of what mistakes or blind workings of Fate you would die—and so to leave Faisal behind when he fell under the shrapnel from a rocket burst fired by a low sweeping Mirage with the Star of David painted on its wings was simpler for them, inured to their own imminent deaths, than such a callous act would have been for Faisal. For Faisal had volunteered to fight, he had not volunteered to die, and it was the tension between these two propositions that kept him staring so fixedly down at the three bodies covered with green canvas.

*　　*　　*

The refugees from Gaza, Jerusalem, and the towns of the West Bank could die slowly in the camps, or speedily with Al Fatah. Made desperate by the Jews, they had no choice but to fight, while for Faisal it had been a luxury that had driven him into Al Fatah. It was a gesture of penance for four idle years spent in the university while his fellow refugees suffered in the camps.

Nine months earlier he had been cramming for the entrance examinations of the Faculty of Law at the American University of Beirut, when one night Aisa Touhanie, his roommate, changed the course of both their lives by taking him to a rally outside the university gates for the Palestinian relief fund. After the speeches and the singing they went to a secret Fatah meeting in the refugee camp at Sarhoud, within the city limits. It was the first time in four years that Faisal had been among his own people, and in that sudden shock of recognition he felt himself swept up in such an unexpected shame, an anger so cleansing and right, that when the call for volunteers came he found himself on his feet.

With a shock he realized that he was joining Al Fatah, that he was leaving his idle student's life behind.

"Hurrah! It is for the death!" Aisa had shouted, but Faisal remembered more a slender youth who had cried out, "No, no, it is for the orange trees of Haifa that we fight, not for death!"

In the morning, back in his quarters in the university, Faisal awoke in a somewhat cooler mood, at first dismayed to realize that he had sealed his fate. He looked around the familiar walls. Through a wide dormer window there was a view of cypress gardens and spacious lawns that rolled down to the Mediterranean. Above him the English Renaissance clock tower of the library

chimed out the hour, while on the Rue Bliss, a block behind the university gate, he heard the tram cars clanging
past Uncle Sam's, the "Little America" of bookstores,
bars, and shoeshine stands on Jeanne d'Arc. No more
these easy surroundings for him; no more the luxury of
forgetfulness. He had volunteered in a moment of passion, but he honored his word nevertheless, and he rose
and packed all his worldly belongings in a battered cardboard suitcase, the last relic of his life in the camps. By
that evening he had resigned his seat in his class, turned
in his cards to the Bursar, and walked out through the
high iron gates alone, expecting to be with Al Fatah by
morning.

Instead, it took five months of waiting and pleading
and arguing, for whatever Fatah needed—better equipment, money, an Act of God—it did not need more recruits. For every man killed within the homeland twenty
such as Aisa and Faisal came forward to take his place.
Faisal, in his youthful ardor, had never thought of such
an eventuality. His decision had swept over him too suddenly for rational thought, and he found, having made
the ultimate sacrifice, that his first lesson was humility.

He thought that he had gone to war, and now he
learned that war was waiting. For five months Faisal
marked time, letting men die in sufficient numbers to allow him to serve in their place. Often, walking past the
pink stone walls of the university, his spirits sank. Why
had he thrown everything away? Could he not have
served the cause of his people better as a lawyer than a
fighter? Was all his education for nothing, to be rendered equivalent to a peasant by the blind judgment of a
bullet? If it was justice they sought, justice, after all, re-
quired law.

But such arguments, which would have weighed heavily with him once, now seemed hollow. They reflected a colonial mentality, and Faisal turned away in self-contempt. One moment he had been a diligent student—the next, as if rudely awakened from a dream of Augustan order, he found himself half a century beyond the liberal ideas of the university, beyond compromise and discourse and the illusion of reason. How quaint the nostalgic notion seemed now that men, or nations, were governed by laws! The Zionists would not talk. They had not talked in 1948, but secretly armed themselves with Messerschmitt 109's, tanks, and European arms to drive his people out of Palestine. They had not talked in 1956, but attacked without warning, conspiring with the colonialist enemies of the Arab peoples, Britain and France. In 1967 their only language, sanctioned by the world, was a relentless war of territorial conquest. So, Faisal thought bitterly, escaping the university precincts, turning his back on its implicit lie, let it be relentless war!

Standing idly before the tree-shaded cafés on the Avenue Hamra, his hands thrust deep into empty pockets, his clothing becoming worn and shabby, Faisal felt for the first time what it was to be a refugee in the capital. He learned what it was to be despised. Police who would never have bothered him as a student now told him roughly to move on. Tourists stared at him. In the afternoons he found himself wandering again in the university quarter, watching the students pour out through the gates and run for the trams. Somnambulists, he thought, and turned away. At times he was bitter and depressed. At other times he felt as if a new light had dawned. His desire to act grew stronger, but until Al Fatah called him he could only stand idly before tobacconists', unable to afford a newspaper, soothing his chafed spirits by reading the front-page accounts of guerrilla raids.

A Palestinian refugee himself, Faisal had been carried out of the lost homeland in his mother's arms when he was three years old. He grew up in the relief camp at Sidon. At the age of ten he went to the UNWRA school. When he was eighteen, having distinguished himself in his studies, he won an AID scholarship from the American Embassy—the price, he knew even then, of silence. Now, at twenty-two, he had thrown it over to fight for the cause of his exiled people; yet, if his act was morally right, there still came hours when, watching the students passing freely through the university gates, he was overcome with bewilderment.

Feeling the shabbiness of his clothing, he turned away, afraid of what he might hear.

"You see over there? Across the street? That's Faisal Ajran. He was going to Fatah, now look at him!"

They would laugh, and why not? He wondered if there could really be any hope in such a cause. Had he sacrificed his future for nothing? How many besides himself really cared? It was the unequal contest of David and Goliath, and now the Jew was Goliath.

In this Faisal took comfort from Aisa, whose convictions were stronger than his own. Many nights they walked the cramped, filthy quarter of refugees within the city. Sarhoud was a squalid sector of tin shacks, without running water or electricity, within full view of the tourist hotels at Rousha where the Americans and French sunbathed on balconies. Faisal's anger was rekindled. Twenty years, he thought, twenty years of exile and false promises and Herculean patience and still this. *This*. If his people could wait for twenty years, he would learn to wait patiently for his shadow comrade in Fatah to meet his death. Against all reason, he would choose this fight. The spectacle of tourists photographing the refugee camp from chartered buses (Was it a zoo? Faisal wondered. Are we animals?) made him feel what it was to be Arab, humiliated, stubborn, fanatical.

Yet the university had produced in Faisal a love of Western culture, had developed a nature already sensitive. The Americans had taught him how to think. Why should he deny it? There was a time when he had been grateful. A law degree would have freed him from the hopeless struggle for survival that was the daily fate of his people in the camps. One day it might have taken him to New York, Detroit, or St. Louis. Others had done it. Why shouldn't he? It was necessary only to remain non-political, to remain silent, and to wait assiduously, humbly, on the American Embassy for approval. When you knew what you were escaping, as Faisal did, you could learn to be very silent, very humble. His own family had been driven from their farm near Lake Tiberias, now the possession of a kibbutz of Polish Jews. (And those Jews, those Poles, were socialist! Well, Faisal reflected bitterly, so in their twisted way had been the Nazis!) His mother had died in the refugee camps within the first year. Of his father he remembered little, save the shadow of a broken man, drifting slowly out of his life, sinking into that abyss of wandering poverty, from Beirut, to Damascus, to Amman, out of which such men never returned. Yet of the camp at Sidon, Faisal had a vivid recollection, for he had grown up there a hundred yards from the barbed-wire-guarded oil pipeline through which every hour flowed more wealth, on its way to American pockets, than came to the two thousand families of the camp in a generation. Yes, the Americans had taught him how to think—but toward what end? And for whose benefit? They had attuned his ear to the subtle counterpoint of Bach, Vivaldi, and Mozart, and with dollars in his pocket and a new suit of clothes, sent him to Beirut, half-Catholic, with more churches than mosques, Mediterranean, Latinate, where with his name enrolled in the university chess club, steeped in an atmosphere of Aristotle, Dante, and Locke, he was invited to forget what the camps had been like. What they were still like, after twenty years. What, so far as anyone cared, they would always be like.

They had corrupted him by slow and skillful degrees until at last, in a moment of moral nausea, he had rebelled.

And now he waited.

Until the call to Fatah came, the moment he and Aisa spoke of at supper with a solemn toast to *The Day*, as the Jews of the pale were once said to have furtively whispered *Next Year in Jerusalem*, the two friends, their Embassy stipends cut off, shared a small room with a fellow student in an old building across the Rue Bliss from the university chapel. Behind them, closer at hand, was an old mosque, hardly larger than a tanner's shop, from whose crumbling minaret the muezzin, ascending his wooden parapet to look up at the small square of Allah's blue sky allotted him by the modern buildings, sent forth his hopeless cry to prayer, heeded only by the street sweepers, coffee vendors, the ignorant and the wretched. Faisal watched, possessed by a secret, furtive wish to join them, to reunite himself with the lowliest of his people. Instead, called away from the window by Aisa, he turned back into the room to listen to "The Voice of the Storm," the radio broadcast of Al Fatah from transmitters in Cairo and Baghdad. A political talk had been interrupted by a reading of Persian poetry.

"Do you hear that?" Aisa said, his eyes gleaming. "They're sending a coded message to Fatahs with the people in the occupied territory. Think of it!"

But when the broadcast was over Aisa's spirits fell. He brooded restlessly over the propaganda leaflets that lay scattered on the table. Those of the fanatical Syrian guerrilla organizations he especially despised.

"The Syrian isn't civilized at all," he said gloomily. "He's the descendant of nomads, he's still a camel driver. What have we in common with him? You can smell him a mile off! We Levantines have always been seamen and bankers. Your Egyptian is a farmer, and steady. And the Jordanians, at least, are good soldiers—but the Syrian is a barbarian!"

Antonious, their roommate, objected. "You can't mean that. You're generalizing. Why, look at Damascus."

Aisa turned on him irritably. "Listen, puppy, if the Syrian ever breaks into Palestine he'll kill more Palestinians than Jews. He's worse than Dayan! For half a century he's itched to burn his way to the sea."

Antonious looked to Faisal for support. "But that's all nonsense! You've got that idea because you only listen to Fatah radio. If you want to know what's really going on, look at the PLO pamphlets. A serious man has got to do more than listen to 'The Storm.' "

Antonious, himself a frail Iraqi and no fighter, hesitated guiltily when he saw the look on Aisa's face.

"Who's a man? What are you saying?"

"Even if I'm only a student. I have a right to my opinions."

"Take your opinions!" cried Aisa. "Who else would

want your opinions? You sit in lectures and talk politics, while we who are in Fatah *act!* Listen to 'The Storm.' It's Fatah, and no one else, that understands the people."

"You aren't in Fatah yet," Antonious said timidly.

Unexpectedly, Aisa burst out laughing. "A fair hit, puppy! You don't have to be afraid of us—and in a few weeks we'll be dead. Is that it? I'm sick of listening to little Arabs talk about liberation. You've been talking about it since Lawrence. It's nothing new."

"But did you ever hear it explained before by Arab scholars?" asked Antonious eagerly. "In the past all we got was a Western intellectual or journalist weeping now and then about the wrongs suffered by the Arab peoples. When a Westerner says that, he's nothing but an oddity. And you know what they call him? An anti-Semite!"

Aisa turned angrily. "As if we were not also Semites!"

"Yes," observed Faisal, "and being treated like it, too."

Antonious was puzzled. "You mean it's a civil war?"

"What did you say? What was that? Why, you puppy—do I look like a *zhid?* I'll throw you out the window!"

In the crowded room Faisal and Aisa became the focal point for students drawn from every faculty, lured by their example as if through their eyes they might catch a glimpse into the house of the dead. Long into the hot summer nights, through the cigarette smoke and dim lamplight, they argued over the possibility of liberation. The intellectual sides were endless. There were radical Ba'athists, communists, Nasserites, socialists, old-fashioned Shi'ite Moslems, each with their viewpoint to advance, their objections to raise, their cause to win. Kuwaiti and Saudi Arabian fought Lebanese and Jordanian; Iraqi and Egyptian fought Syrian and Libyan. No action was possible until all theoretical considerations had been settled. It was the old, corrupt genius of the Arab race for argument. In these skirmishes Aisa launched himself avidly, striking out in every direction in defense of Fatah, while Faisal, withdrawn into a dark corner of the room, felt himself losing all patience. Once he had been like this, in love with rhetoric, mistaking words for reality. Now he understood that these students were the death of Islam.

"What we need is action," he shouted angrily, leaping to his feet, "not mere words! We have been choking on words for fifty years!"

Startled, he realized that he had repeated the doctrine of Al Fatah—*Victory first, politics second.* Abashed at his own ardor, he said nothing more, though months later, caught up in the wordless agony of physical exhaustion, crawling on his face under the coils of barbed wire, learning how to load and fire an AK-47 while lying on his side, how to fuse and plant land mines, he thought back to those last nights of wild, foolish, beautiful students' talk as the sweetest of his life. He did not hate them for it; he did not even waste time pitying them; he only hoped they would quickly open their eyes to the real world. Yet in his tent at night, still with Aisa and four other recruits, taciturn, half-literate peasants, he would feel a deep homesickness for the university, for it was not just friends, but a civilization, that he had left behind. He wondered if he would ever be able to trade this dust and sweat and anger for the rhythms of Vivaldi and Mozart. Was there still, somewhere, he wondered, a world of *The Magic Flute?* Did men of good will still listen to *The Seasons?* His mind seemed to drift, lost between two loyalties: the one Western, affluent, safe—the

16

other Arabic, poor, fatalistic. At such moments, by an
act of will, he brought his divided mind back to the tent,
to cleaning his Chinese AK-47 attack rifle, to breaking
apart, cleaning, assembling, and breaking apart again his
automatic pistol, a 7.62 mm Czechoslovakian weapon that
he could now fire accurately at a range of two hundred
yards. These things, the socialist weapons, were real. The
world of civilized discourse was an illusion. Observing
the stolid manners of the peasant recruits he felt deeply
rebuked, for here were the true sons of Islam, patient,
long-suffering, and determined, ready to die with a clear
conscience and commend their souls to Allah. Could he
say as much for himself? No, all this, the consolation of
faith, had been taken from him; this deep solace of
thoughtlessness would never be his. He had sold his birth-
right for the pale light of Reason, and now he would have
to live and die with only that fragile hope. He thought
with a shudder how far toward the West he had been
lured, how far the university had altered—even now, he
could not bring himself to say corrupted—his mind. He
remembered the dark-eyed girls in the sweet shops of
Beirut, the young men of his generation standing at the
bar in Uncle Sam's or waiting idly on street corners with
one foot on a shoeshine stand and a cigarette dangling
from their lips, presenting their profiles to traffic in imita-
tion of Belmondo, Camus, Hemingway. He remembered
the facile, empty wit of the students strolling arm in arm
along the Avenue de Paris on a balmy summer's evening,
the quiet Mediterranean and their whole empty lives outstretched before them, on their way to spend the night
talking politics in Chez Popeye. For to argue politics, he
thought, was the last consolation of the oppressed, the one
right which their masters willingly left them. Remem-

bering so much, he was content to crawl wordlessly under the barbed-wire entanglements, cutting himself and
swearing furiously at the live ammunition that whined
over his head, for those .50-caliber machine gun bullets
were utterly indifferent to his fate. They were blind to
history, unmoved by rhetoric. You wish to stand up?
Would you like to raise a final point of order? Perhaps
you have one last objection? Very well, we will cut you
down and give your place to another! Faisal found something profoundly satisfying in those kinetic chunks of
lead that ripped the air apart over his trembling shoulders
as he crawled through the training course, physically
humbled, his mouth full of the same dust that choked the
peasant at his side, for they said, If you want to serve, be
silent and go forward! It was as simple as that—go forward, or die! Here was a clear answer. Here was the ultimate rebuttal, the tactic, unforeseen, suicidal, and fanatical, for which the enemy had no answer, and Faisal
yielded himself with all his heart to the crude temptation
of the act against the subtlety of the word, for when
they found human flesh were not each of these .50-
caliber bullets, quite literally, worth a lifetime of talk?

Then Faisal was thankful not to be walking the tree-
shaded paths of the university in the company of those
almond-eyed girls. He hoped never again to see Chez
Popeye. There had been no future for him there; there
was only the death of whatever it was that he, Faisal Abu
Ajran, had been born to be. He would relearn what it
was to be Arab and most likely, he knew, for this heresy
he would die. On the gunnery range he sometimes
glimpsed Aisa nearby, and between them would pass a
thrill of recognition that made him want to leap to his
feet to shout for joy. But the joy, and the novelty of

weapons, was beaten out of him by the first week's training. The secret camp to which they were sent was hidden in a rocky valley less than a mile from the Israeli border. Sometimes, at night, they could see the flash of artillery duels between the Israeli and Jordanian batteries behind Shitar el Eid, hear the moan of the shells passing overhead. The flashes rippled on the horizon like heat lightning, and slowly the rumble of the heavy guns rolled over the camp, as somnolent as thunder. There, like the waiting sacrifice to some God with an unappeasable appetite for human flesh, Faisal and the four peasant recruits waited through the night in their tent, without a light, wondering when they would be called upon to cross the Jordan into enemy-held territory. Aisa, distinguishing himself in training, had already been sent twice. From him Faisal learned all the nightmare mementos of war, the mistaken direction taken in pitch blackness, the mine fields, the electric warning fences, of never quite knowing when one of the ripples of light on the horizon was the one that would seal your fate. Then, at last, Faisal went out. He was ordered to plant a mine on a road a mile inside the occupied territory. He went alone, tested by a guerrilla army that knew it could afford to sacrifice men, that behind every Faisal there waited a dozen replacements. But Faisal came back without difficulty, never to know the effect of his mine, and that night he dreamt of tropic islands, of Paris and New York and the mazurkas of Chopin danced by girls on the beach, and he found, when he awoke the next morning in the hard desert light, that he could now shake off these childish things with a practiced shrug.

He felt himself at last a Fatah, an instrument in the hands of the people.

Two Camps

HE had been the first to hear the truck from Golan bringing in their dead, and the five survivors, and had risen from his cot and stood at the open flap of the tent. All morning his thoughts had been preoccupied. Aisa had been gone for two nights, out somewhere on a mission deep inside Israel, and Hamad, Deeb, Khalid, the other members of his squad, had been resting on their heels, eating peasant-fashion, when the truck's engine was heard whining in low gear up the hill from the left, in the direction of the river. Moments later it rattled into camp over the corrugated-metal pontoon bridge, clattering like a railway car crossing a trestle. After the five survivors had piled out and collected their gear, the squad leader went in to make his report to the Major. The covered bodies were still in the truck.

In the blazing noonday heat the air was absolutely still. Only the metallic clink of Hamad's fork on his mess kit broke the silence. A vague instinct told Faisal to look up.

There, in a transparent sky, twin jet contrails were streaking eastward—Israeli fighters. They were too high to be heard, two pencil-thin white lines being drawn out against the deep blue vault of the heavens. A ruffle of hot wind flapped the walls of the tent, contracting them like a lung and expanding them slowly. Faisal watched as a detail of recruits went down to remove the bodies from the truck, then he started for the Major's command post.

Inside the dark, stucco room the leader of the decimated patrol, Abdullah, was making his report. He sat on a wooden bench, rubbing his face roughly as if to dispel some lingering web of thought, some doubt of his own right actions during the patrol that had run into such trouble. In the large room there were half a dozen other men, all of them fighters, save for one, a tall American journalist, Robert Shoemaker, whom Faisal had seen coming and going in the camp for a week. The sunlight in the open doorway was so intense that it burned white. Objects melted into it; vision blurred into mirages. Over his shoulder, from time to time, Faisal looked out at the distant bodies, which were now being laid out on the ground like cut wood. Behind him he heard the Major encouraging Abdullah.

"Good, good, you hurt them! There was nothing mistaken in your plan. You must steel yourself."

"I am sorry that we could not bring out little Samir," Abdullah said.

The Major shook his head slowly. "Let the Jew keep the dead. They have their own." He glanced toward the open door, as if listening for the far-off sounds of aerial bombardment. "And in a few minutes we will have more than we need."

Everyone who had seen the jets knew what they were

for, though it was a good ten minutes before Captain Ali, the square-shouldered regular, came down from the radio shack. In the June War he had been a captain in the Jordanian army. His company had held its ground doggedly for five days, though hit with everything the Jews could find to throw at it. When the Amman government gave up the struggle he resigned his commission in disgust and came to Fatah as a common soldier. A professional, he seldom spoke, though when he did he was listened to with respect. Among the guerrillas he was known as "*Al Sakhr*," the Rock, the one who would not yield. He nodded briefly to Faisal, and handed in a note.

"For the Major," he said, still speaking in the formal third-person usage which the British had drilled into him, and which, to Faisal, sounded jarringly out of place in a guerrilla command post.

Kassim looked up without bothering to take the note. "The reprisal?" he asked.

Ali nodded curtly. "They have attacked with American Skyhawk fighter bombers against the base camp at Deir al Quamar."

"Ah!" said the Major with evident satisfaction. "They are up early this morning!" He turned to Robert Shoemaker. "The Jew is like a frog with its brain excised—shock it in the right place, and the leg kicks. A matter of reflex, nothing more. The Jew thinks that he decides when he will strike, but it is *we* who decide. Frogs are predictable." Then, turning to Ali: "Is there much damage?"

"They used napalm," said the Captain. "Three passes were made on the fuel dump before the antiaircraft could come into action." The Major smiled grimly; everyone in the room knew that the antiaircraft were obsolete machine guns mounted on truck beds. "The anti-aircraft," continued Ali dryly, "was then knocked out. The section leader, Braheim, says there is heavy damage. We are warned," he concluded, "to take precautions."

The Major glanced at Robert Shoemaker to see if he appreciated the full irony of this: first, that the enemy jets had struck Deir al Quamar in reprisal for the raid which had come from their own camp, El Husn; secondly, the mordant humor, whether intended or not, of advising them to take precautions. Kassim looked at Faisal, who nodded uneasily to acknowledge that, yes, he had seen the jets which had streaked high over the camp a few minutes before. Faisal had thought it not worth while to report them, for anyone within twenty miles could have seen them for himself. If they had been after El Husn they would not have come over so high, they would have crossed the river low and fast, striking at hill-top level before there could have been any warning. Against such air attacks, in desert hill country devoid of cover, one simply took one's chances in the open. There were no precautions. If the Jew hurt you because you had blown up a pumping station, the next night you, or whoever was still alive, went back and blew up two pumping stations. It was as simple as that.

The Major turned back to Ali. "What are the casualties at Al Quamar?" he asked.

"There is a settlement of West Bank refugees over there, most of them evacuees from the June War," Ali replied. "They were hit with napalm, along with the fuel dump, which was nearby. As to the camp, it will take them awhile to dig themselves out. Then they will know how many fighters they have lost."

The Major swung about in his chair, looking intently

at a wall map of Palestine. The American newspaperman looked up, waiting for him to speak, though the rest of them understood that no such pronouncement as Shoemaker expected was coming. Kassim was not a man of easy declarations. He was a calculator, who smoked American cigarettes and played the American game, poker. He looked at the little flags stuck on the map, red for the Fatah camps, blue for Israeli outposts across the river. Then he turned to gaze toward the white rectangle of the door with a perfectly quiet, unaffected ease, so steady that Faisal himself, though long accustomed to the Major's habits, wondered if the fate of napalm victims at Deir al Quamar meant anything to him at all. Yet he did not want to believe the Major callous, for his own life depended on him. Rather, he told himself, watching Kassim with the awed fascination he might have felt for an actor entering upon the first motions of a great and difficult part, this insouciance, which looked so inhuman, was the iron self-control and habitual caution of an old political officer, a revolutionary who had for two decades conspired in bars and planted mines in cafés until at last, like a gift from Allah, the utter collapse of the discredited Arab armies had brought forth the inevitable doctrine of Al Fatah, and with it the rise to political authority of theoreticians like himself. He did not think in terms of tanks, infantry regiments, aircraft, artillery, or logistics (those children's games, taught at staff colleges, played on maps), but of the new warfare, learned in the streets of Baghdad and Damascus, the subtle, indestructible weapons of propaganda, world opinion, endurance, will power. Did Robert Shoemaker think that these Israeli jets could affect the outcome of the struggle? Well, he might ask the citizens of Hanoi! Let them blow up fuel dumps. Let them burn a handful of men. The supplies of both were inexhaustible. Such attacks, far from alarming Kassim, struck him as futile. From the vantage of Fatah doctrine, each reprisal of the Jew was an Arab victory. But even if he had been alarmed, Kassim would not have allowed himself to move without this moment of deliberation. This composure of his, this reflex of thought, was a defense which he had learned in the underground, in those clandestine struggles where one's innermost motives had to be kept secret even from one's comrades if they were not to be betrayed. Hiding for so many years, could he now, Faisal wondered, a little awestruck, be expected to display himself for something as trivial as an air raid?

The Major looked up at Ali, one eyebrow raised interrogatively. "Is that all?" he asked.

Ali's heels came together, the reflex of long military duty. "Yes."

"Well," he said, "well."

The small delicate hands worked into the khaki shirt pocket for a pack of cigarettes, a match was struck, the cigarettes replaced in the pocket (the brand, Faisal noticed, as if by deliberate irony, was Lucky Strike), and the shirt flap carefully rebuttoned. To Faisal these slow motions inspired more confidence than the bravest words. Were they about to be hit at El Husn? Should they order a general dispersal of the camp until after dark? What of the vital equipment? No, it was not Kassim's military knowledge that made men follow him—Ali and a dozen others far surpassed him in this. With a sudden flash of insight, not unlike gratitude, Faisal understood that what gave the Major the right to command was his ability to remain unmoved and to think cold-

bloodedly in a crisis. The Israeli Air Force, the best tacti-
cally in the world, struck, and you did not run. Thus
you showed the Jew that your death meant nothing to
the struggle. Victory was inevitable in any case. Above
all else, the Major taught them how to die, for you feared
death less when it did not bring the sting of defeat. Even
when he had turned to smile at Robert Shoemaker to
show that he was pleased that their raid on Kibbutz
Sha'al had stung the Jew enough to provoke this swift
retaliatory strike, it had been a careful, self-aware smile.
Even then, with bombs falling at Deir al Quamar, Major
Kassim was a political officer, a poker player, an actor.

Captain Ali waited, meanwhile, with visible impatience, his military bearing in strong opposition to the
Major's slumped shoulders. He stared down at him, waiting for orders, and slowly a deep frown appeared between his large, dark eyes. Faisal felt the danger of Ali's
mounting disapproval of the Major's silence, throbbing
around them in the room like a heartbeat, while the
Major studied the view of stone, sun-baked earth, and
the slice of blue sky visible through the doorway. The
others orbited like satellites around him in the command
post: Ali, the spurned, official slip of paper still in his
hand; Abdullah, who was looking down at his boots, his
eyes nearly closed with fatigue; the other fighters; Robert Shoemaker; himself. From the back of the camp,
against the rocky hillside, came the staccato snap of small
arms fire on the gunnery range.

Ten minutes were passed in this silence, as if cast in
amber. At last Kassim stirred. The two Israeli jets, for
whatever reason, had left El Husn for another time.

"Go to your men and sleep," he said, turning to Abdullah, shattering the fragile web which his immobility

had woven around them all. "Eat something if you can. When your stomach is full you will think differently about things."

Abdullah was too exhausted to reply. Kassim turned to the radioman.

"Raise Deir al Quamar now. It is time I spoke to Braheim, if he is still alive."

When the Major picked up the headset Faisal for the first time saw the other camp not as an abstract fact under the title "air strike," but as it actually was—the burning, overturned vehicles, the gutted buildings, shrill cries of wounded men and women, bodies lying charred beyond recognition in the indifferent sunlight. Were there really West Bank families over there? Why had they located in a military camp? He felt suddenly weak. The losses, he gathered, listening to Kassim, had been larger than first thought, but Braheim was alive. His voice burst forth through the static of the radio. Kassim spoke calmly, reassuring his counterpart.

"Do you need anything?" Faisal heard him ask. "Keep your voice down, they will hear you—Braheim, do you understand? Keep your voice down! Calm yourself. You must be firm."

All this was spoken with the detachment of a man who had seen too much carnage to have any feelings left, yet to whom, in some difficult moment of street fighting a decade before had been given the title "The Liberator." As Faisal watched, Kassim seemed to become old and wizened, listening silently to whatever tale of horror Braheim was delivering, and a bitter look entered his otherwise neutral eyes. He could not hide his weariness with these others whose vision of the Holy City wavered with every blow of the enemy. Calmly, he heard Braheim out; calmly, he restored his confidence, made him see the victory in this defeat, returned him to the narrow path of his peculiar salvation. Like a priest in the confessional, he took the sins of disbelief from his double at Al Quamar, managed to touch him somehow with his iron will. He had been the Liberator for a decade, without a nerve in his body, and though he was not yet fifty it had made him old, patient, and unswerving. Faisal had heard it said that Kassim, in one way or another, had been directly responsible for the violent deaths of over seven hundred men, women, and children. All that saved Kassim in his own eyes was that, in each case, he had been politically right. History was the revolutionary's God, and while the Major spoke his carefully chosen, deliberate words into the microphone, Faisal felt, with a shiver, whether of horror or admiration he could not have said, that he thus heard History pronounce the deaths at Deir al Quamar a victory.

Kassim returned his attention to the command post, and to Ali, who shared, along with Robert Shoemaker, some special immunity; he could openly doubt with the security of a favored infidel where none of the rest of them would have dared. For Robert Shoemaker, this immunity was due to his propaganda value as a newspaperman (Kassim would take the tall American to Al Quamar; the charred bodies of a woman and her child would appear the next night in half the world's newspapers; the stomach, and therefore the conscience, of mankind would turn over). For Ali, heresy was permissible because the Major could not do without his military knowledge, perhaps also because, whatever he might think of the Captain's political orthodoxy, he could not ignore his conduct during the June War. Here, at least, was a man as stubborn as himself, an Arab soldier who would not run.

"Well, Captain?" he asked, regarding him with a look which was largely the condescension of an adult for a willful child.

Ali drew himself up. "Does the Major still want the Beit Shal operation for tonight?"

Kassim turned slowly in his seat, carefully replacing the radio headset. "Yes," he said, "nothing has changed. You will take your men across three miles below Mokhtara. You should be in place by 1800."

Ali's face was expressionless. "After Deir al Quamar, the Jews will be expecting us."

Kassim smiled slightly. "Well, we don't want to disappoint them, Captain."

"There won't be any element of surprise," Ali said stubbornly. "That increases the risk."

"Surprise? At Mokhtara, no. A mile or two anywhere inside the frontier, no. They will be waiting for us to strike a dozen places across the river." Kassim frowned. "But they will not be waiting for you at Beit Shal."

"If we get through," Ali said.

"You will get through! We owe it to the Jew. I have already told you that."

"Fifteen miles into enemy territory and back, in nine hours, is just barely possible in the most theoretical sense. If anything goes wrong," Ali warned, "*anything*, there will be absolutely no chance of getting the squad out. Not tonight."

The Major's face changed. The smile vanished, replaced by a veiled, ominous look.

"Does the Captain want me to assign someone else to lead the raid on Beit Shal? Perhaps Abdullah here, or Dr.

Rashid? Or would you prefer Faisal?"

He asked his taunting question slowly, speaking for effect not on Ali, who was immovable, and who would obey in any case, but on the half dozen others who stood watching. The very neutrality of the Major's tone lent to the question all the threatening innocence of a public prosecutor about to destroy an unwary witness. The command post took on the thunderous silence of an interrogation room. Very slowly, Kassim took out a handkerchief and wiped his forehead, his throat, then, methodically, his hands. A fly droned over the radio, furnishing the only sound in the room. Outside the open door the August sun blazed on the flat ground, the stones shivered in its heat. Inside the sweltering hut the damp odor of rotting stucco mingled with human sweat and kerosene. Slowly, Kassim put his handkerchief away.

"I will lead my squad," Ali said, looking down at the Major, "but it's farther than we have ever gone from El Husn before, and the conditions are not proper. That's all I say."

"Conditions are never proper!" Kassim snapped. "Neither for us, nor the Jew. He doesn't have men enough to be everywhere at once. You will get through without question." He regarded Ali as if he had forgotten the most elementary fact of guerrilla warfare—the risks of improvised raids against an entrenched and mechanized enemy. "Are your plans ready?"

"For two weeks."

"You know your route?"

"Perfectly."

"And the target?"

"Yes."

"Then it is time we went to Beit Shal!" Kassim said.

"It is time we put out the lights." Bemused, mysterious, wrapped again in solitude, he regarded the map while in the silence the radio whined; behind the hill someone squeezed off three rounds from a light machine gun, then three more, again three. Kassim studied the map for a moment longer, considering; then he turned to Robert Shoemaker, who had risen to go to the water cooler.

"I have been thinking lately, Shoemaker, my friend," the Major said. "I have been considering. I have been thinking of our individual group, and of Al Fatah as a whole. I asked myself, 'What opinion does the Jew have of us?' I mean, what kind of adversary does he think he faces? Does he fear us? Does he understand more now than he did in 1967? How does he think our minds work? I considered what his answers might be, and I tried to listen very carefully to what he had to say." Kassim paused, tapping his fingertips together before his face, his eyes bright and lips pursed, as if he were indeed projecting himself into the mind of his enemy. Robert Shoemaker was listening; he watched Kassim with eyes that equaled his own for patience. Against the thumb of his left hand there was the button of a miniature tape recorder, which he now pushed. Satisfied, the Major continued. "Unhappily," he said, "I reached this conclusion: the Jew still does not understand. He is not yet afraid. Like all people with strong backs, he has a thick skull. I am sure that you will agree that throughout history his greatest mistake has been his contempt for his enemies. There alone is he vulnerable! Only in his arrogance is he weak! He imagines," he said, turning briefly toward Ali with a thin smile at the absurdity of the military mind, "that it is still a matter of tanks and flame throwers and bombardments. We must teach him otherwise." Kassim lit another cigarette from the butt of the old one, chain-smoking with steady hands. "The Jew is feeling secure, fighting only on his own borders, fighting only where it pleases him. Why not? He has nothing to lose. Thus far we have been gentle with him. He has been made complacent. That is why he is vulnerable at Beit Shal. We have taught him the rules for one kind of fighting, now we will teach him another. We are the fish that swim in the people, are we not? So then, let us swim! What is your opinion, Mr. Shoemaker?"

"No doubt you are right, Major Kassim. Of course," he added, "there will be more reprisals."

"It is what we want."

"I understand."

"Up till now we have fought with only our left hand." Kassim smiled, clenching one fist, then the other. "We, too, have been learning. Now we will fight with both! The Jew is standing on the border? We will hit him deep in his own territory. When he covers himself there, we will hit him on the border. He does not have enough men to defend himself everywhere at once. He has swallowed too much territory. We will keep hitting him until he begins to understand that!" The Major looked up with confidence. "What do you say to that, Captain? Shall we go to Beit Shal tonight, or not?"

Surprised, Faisal heard Ali continue to object stubbornly.

"Fifteen miles is too far," Ali went on doggedly, "especially on the return. The enemy may not expect us at Beit Shal, but once we strike he'll cover every foot of the way out. I don't want anyone with me who does not volunteer. We may not be able to cross the river before daylight, and in that case . . ."

"My dear Captain, there is a flaw in your thinking that is not characteristic of you." Again Kassim's tone was patient and forgiving as if he were speaking to a child. "I know everything of your conduct during the June War. You occupied Hill 203, outside Jerusalem, with one reinforced company against the attack of an entire battalion of Jewish infantry. You had four jeeps with recoilless rifles; the Jew had armored halftracks, American tanks, flame throwers, and absolute air superiority. Now then, Captain, you remained on that hilltop for one hundred and twenty hours, while the rest of the Jordanian army crumbled around you. May I ask why? When the Jew infantry attacked, you stopped them, one foot at a time. Again, I ask *why?* When the King ordered you to retreat, you refused. Your position was pounded with howitzers and mortars, and you dug deeper. Then their airplanes dropped napalm, and half your men burned to death. Those who were still alive kept fighting. When the cease-fire was ordered by King Hussein you were still on that hilltop, surrounded by a sea of Jew infantry and armor. Now then, Captain, all of this is known. You wanted to fight. Was that not why you stayed on Hill 203? You were not defeated, but betrayed! Now I ask you which is better, to be trapped outside Jerusalem on a burning hill, or to be deep in the Promised Land, at night, able to strike swiftly on your own terms, and knowing that at the very least for every Arab who dies a Jew will also die?" Kassim leaned forward dramatically, jabbing the air with his pencil. "Captain, was this not why you joined Al Fatah—to *fight?*"

Ali remained silent, as if to answer were beneath him.

Satisfied, Kassim visibly relaxed, his eyes almost unnervingly tranquil. His smile was not unfriendly. "On

Hill 203 you were expendable for nothing but military stupidity. Here you are expendable in a cause worthy of your death." Kassim's smile tightened, and he leaned forward still farther, in a half gesture of conciliation—something—it was impossible to separate the man from the actor. "But Captain, you are *expendable* nevertheless."

Ali smiled grimly. "I will not die," he said. "Not yet. Not tonight."

"Good! Good!" The Major stood up, embracing the Captain, whose opposition he had neutralized. Was Kassim an actor, Faisal wondered, a man whose deepest motives would never be known? Or was he merely a man with a fixed vision (himself a slave) to which all other men must be brought into accord? They fought; therefore they died! The litany had been restored to its proper formula. You did not ask how difficult it might be to get out from Beit Shal, how ill-chosen this troubled night might be—that was what the Jew expected you to ask, why, as the Major had said, he felt secure at Beit Shal and every other stolen village on the West Bank, and exactly why he was vulnerable there, because it was too far, it was not humanly possible, because you could not get out alive. Instead, you asked where your possible death would hurt the enemy most, and then, surely with no more tenacity than had made Ali stick to his burning hilltop outside Jerusalem, you went forward with no thought of personal danger. All of this burned now in the eyes of the young men with an almost religious anger, and they rose to their feet; Robert Shoemaker's tape recorder was still turning, awaiting the Major's final words of exhortation. But Kassim disappointed them all. With the theatrical timing of an old actor, he left the scene suspended, unfinished, ready to play again. He took out his crumpled handkerchief and wiped his sweating brow, looking far less like a prophet than a small and unremarkable, long-suffering man scarred by fate and shackled to history.

His words to Ali were simple: "I believe, Captain, that you need replacements."

Ali nodded, as if the Major had anticipated his next question. "Two of my men were lost with Abdullah last night."

"Very well, take Faisal with you," the Major said, "and his friend Hamad. They have worked together, and if your group is separated they will know what to do. You have all you need to accomplish what I want?"

"I need only three men."

"Because," said the Major, gripping his arm, "we must make a noise they will hear all the way to Tel Aviv! We must not let them relax for a second!" He turned to the radioman. "If you can contact Amman, tell them that we plan Mokhtara for tonight. Put it on the air clear. Also raise Deir al Quamar as often as you can; keep them talking. And tell them to send a patrol down along the river. I want the Jew to see them." He went to the door. "Come with me, if you please, Shoemaker, my friend. You can hear what Abdullah's men have to say about last night. I have no doubt," he said, without the least outward sign of irony, "that it will make good copy for you." Without looking back he spoke to Ali. "Send Dr. Rashid over to Deir al Quamar with as many men as he needs. Tell him to use my jeep. If he wishes, he can have an ambulance truck, though," he added, "if they have used napalm, he is not going to have much to piece together. In the meantime we must see what we can do for Deir al Quamar. It would be a pity, but convenient nevertheless," he said, turning to the journalist, "if the Jew has killed a few women and children."

"Let us hope not," said Robert Shoemaker.

The Major shrugged. "That is up to the Jew."

There was a general exodus from the room. Ali detained Abdullah, laying his big hand on his shoulder.

"What happened last night?"

"I don't know," Abdullah said, looking up with relief now that the Major had gone. "We took a wrong turn. You know what those gulleys are at night. And then with the Jews at your heels . . . At sunrise we still had a mile to go to the river. It was too far. They had patrols and a helicopter after us." He shrugged. "We were waist-deep in the water when it caught us."

"Better try to sleep," Ali advised.

"I can't. Anyway, I've got a brother at Al Quamar. I'm going over there." Abdullah's eyes were sunken and dull. He looked hard, sullen, and bitter. He had, as Faisal watched, reached the point where strong men weep in their worst moments of defeat. What had happened a few hours before, the loss of half his men, was still dawning on him. "Fifteen miles," he said slowly, his eyes outraged as he looked up at Ali, then Faisal, *"fifteen miles. And that's as the crow flies. Why not march all the way to Jerusalem and put a bomb in Dayan's pocket?"

"Why not, indeed?" Ali smiled.

Abdullah subsided weakly, rubbing his face. "He is crazy, you know. Kassim. He is a fanatic."

"Get some rest, Abdullah."

"No," he protested, "I have a brother at Al Quamar." But instead of rising he leaned over the table with his face buried in his arms.

Ali signaled to Faisal and the two of them left Abdullah alone with the radioman in the command post. Outside the air was so heavy that it felt as if they had gone under water. "I'm glad that I'm going with you," Faisal said lamely, constrained by the Captain's silence. The Captain had asked for volunteers; well, thought Faisal, he would let him know that he came of his own free will, not because Kassim had singled him out.

Captain Ali had dark, regular features. No taller than he should have been, he was powerfully built, hard to knock off his feet. Compared to the wrinkled, civilian softness of the Major's face, Ali had something about him, even in his camouflage fatigues, of those Islamic heroes who had once carried the sword and the Koran to half the Mediterranean, carving out an empire from Europe's underbelly that stretched from the gates of Vienna to Roncevalles. Such men as Ali had once held Europe in the palm of their hand. Seen in the operations tent at night, poring over a map under the orange-and-black air-raid light, his somber face deep in concentration as he tried to predict the route and strength of enemy responses, he looked the perfect example of the staff officers of the Arab armies. Yet those armies, Faisal reflected, had failed.

Ali stopped abruptly, squinting at Faisal as though he were crazy. "Do you know what you're getting into?" he asked.

Faisal's stomach tightened. He said nothing, but looked around the camp. The news of the air strike at Deir al Quamar had spread. Equipment was being hastily loaded onto trucks; the doctor had already left in the Major's jeep. He glanced at Ali. The ex-Jordanian army captain hated Kassim, he suspected, as soldiers must always hate politicians. He himself had no opinion in the

matter, would have said, if pressed, that the cause needed
both; but quickly, with the speed of thought, he calcu-
lated how much danger there might be for Hamad and
himself in the Captain's dislike of Kassim and his obvious
reluctance about the raid. Ali disliked Kassim not because
he thought him dictatorial or a fool, but because Ali had
been bred to the British system of command, because he
was a regular still, and would always be a regular, and
because Kassim, the street agitator, whose skull Ali
would once, on the King's service, gladly have cracked,
now held over Ali exactly that right of command, un-
challenged, unbending, absolute, that only a regular
army major should have possessed. After fifteen years of
army life, Ali would have despised any Fatah chief. With
a soldier's pride he would always in his heart loathe the
guerrillas, and perhaps himself most of all for now being
a guerrilla. When he fought the Israeli regulars, Faisal
wondered, did he see himself in their uniforms, with that
military system of command, that order, that discipline?
Faisal counted on his anger, and his pride, to see them
through. But he wondered who, under his military bearing, Ali hated most—the Jews, or Kassim?

"I know what I'm getting into," said Faisal. "I heard
the Major. We are going to Beit Shal."

"And do you know what that means? I'm not talking
about distances on a map, but on the ground! It's farther
than from here to Marjouyan. We will have to make it at
a forced march, going in, and coming out—no, coming
out, with the Jews after us, we will simply be running for
our lives if we don't want to get caught short of the river
by sunrise. We'll all carry heavy packs of high explosives.
With the time lost in avoiding patrols, and in setting
the fuses, to cover fifteen miles in four hours will be al-

most impossible. Almost. Maybe it will all come right. But I want you to know what is involved here." He regarded Faisal sharply for a moment. "If you don't think you can do it, say so now, or you'll endanger us all. To lie would be stupid."

"I'm young." Faisal grinned. "I can run."

"All right," Ali said. "Tell Hamad to get some rest. You too. I'll give you a briefing at 1500 hours."

"The Major is not a bad man," Faisal called after him, "he's just in a difficult position! After all, we only have to fight; he has to be responsible for everything."

"Precisely," Ali said, and left him.

Faisal was suddenly embarrassed at having spoken to the Captain in such a way. His face flamed. He felt foolish and he knew that what he had said had sounded foolish, but he did not dare to believe the Major wrong when his life depended on his being right. This raid was clearly dangerous, far more dangerous than anything else he had done thus far with Fatah. Compared to it, all his other patrols, the mining of a deserted road, the lying in ambush against a lonely jeep, were the exploits of adolescent boys. He had seen a deep awareness of fear even in Ali's eyes when he spoke of Beit Shal. Faisal shuddered. For the first time his thoughts of Kassim were stained with doubt. Perhaps he was feeling the aftereffects of the two jets he had seen, and what he knew they had done at Al Quamar. Or was it Abdullah, who was only now beginning to realize the full enormity of what had happened to him in the river?

All at once Faisal felt unutterably tired. His mind wandered as if he had not slept for a week. The hard-packed earth, the sharp divisions of light and dark where the shadows of roofs fell across stucco walls, dazzling the eye, the solid, cold dread that had crept into his blood, the white contrails of other jets, perhaps Jordanian now, crossing the sky in another direction, the harsh grinding of trucks moving through the camp—everything accumulated at once to make him feel as if he had walked against a solid wall on a dark night, his sense of direction confused, listening intently for what might lie ahead. University, friends, books—all this came back to him like the far-off memory of some remote light, an inaccessible shore which had never existed at all save in a dream of childish brevity. Months of training had made him feel that all there had ever been in his life was this endless walk from his tent to the rifle range and on to the weary rounds of political lectures, with now and then, at the most unexpected times, a shocking moment of actual combat. Like a man in delirium, he could not say which was real, that past or this present time; all he knew was that he could not exist in both worlds at once. He felt himself hopelessly encircled, befuddled, and directionless in the midst of the blazing, sunlit camp.

Faisal went up to the tent to warn Hamad, but he found him rolled over with his face pressed damply against the rough canvas of his cot, asleep. Feeling bitterly alone, Faisal sat down on his own cot and waited, chilled to the bone despite the furnace heat. Something carried over from the morning, a look on Ali's face, or perhaps that other thing, the sight of the dead bodies being lifted out of the truck, had poisoned his eagerness for this raid (for after all, had he not come to fight, like the Captain? Was this not his greatest chance?) with a cold, persistent fear, or what was worse, something less tangible than fear—an uncertainty, a haunting burden of irrational doubt, all the more menacing for being nameless.

The danger of the raid was obviously great, but training had accustomed him to the feel and use of weapons, and he knew that he was not a coward, yet still the Captain's words (or had it been Kassim's?) left him open to unfamiliar worries, premonitions of disaster. He might have ignored these had the morning not already been so strange, with its truckload of dead, Aisa gone, the faint silver points of jets against a blue sky, so beautiful in their aloof cleanliness, raining down fire and death at Deir al Quamar. Did Abdullah really have a brother over there? Faisal shuddered. He was too young. He felt his own innocence not as a positive quality, a saving grace, but, rather, as ignorance, moral as well as physical, of what this impending night might demand of him. He watched Hamad's heavy, untroubled sleep, his mouth agape, his shoulders rising and falling deeply on each breath. Looking at his tent mate, Faisal was struck by a still deeper sense of alienation, for there, he thought, was the essential difference between them—even if Hamad had known where they were going, he would have slept his indifferent, peasant's sleep.

But fear is a kind of anger, and sitting on his cot, staring out through the sun-scorched triangle of the tent flap and thinking of what lay ahead, Faisal felt suddenly angry and embittered. The Jews, the state of the world, land mines, hand grenades, night ambushes, all these were his natural enemies. These were the things which conspired to sweep him off into oblivion. And he was now, he reflected honestly, a part of the state of the world. He had wanted to protest its injustice, and had succeeded only in making its injustice a part of his life. He was not cynical. The Nazi death camps? Auschwitz, Bergen-Belsen, Treblinka? Yes, he remembered that. There was always that, Faisal admitted—but why should his people have to pay? Was a Jewish tyranny sweeter because the Jews themselves had suffered? Did the German terror justify the Jews in terrorizing the Arabs? Because the Jews, for all Europe owed them, had once lived in Palestine? Well, so had Arabs, and for a great deal longer! Or was it because the Americans had refused to take the Jews after the war, that he, Faisal Abu Ajran, was now told to spend his life rotting in a desert camp? Yes, there was the rub and that other guilt. Unable to decide whom to blame, Faisal drew back from this view of the sheer hellishness of things, of the hopeless tangle of affairs, and made his narrow, human cry—Not us! Not us! Somehow in the turmoil of his thoughts Fatah still lay wrapped with the ideal of justice, which he could not separate from honesty and courage. And that in his time meant only one thing—the struggle to bring the exiles home.

The only way to live was to fight!

Retracing his motives, he sought to calm himself, but something was wrong. The conclusion, once convincing, was hollow; the numbing fear remained. He felt as helpless as a pawn about to be advanced toward its sacrifice by inexplicable forces. If he was not to lose his moorings entirely he would have to hold to what he had left—his attack rifle, knife, automatic pistol, skill in night assault—until it all came right. In his months with Fatah he had crossed the Jordan often enough to have had a taste of that fear of heavy tanks and guns, of the mechanized enemy who killed you swiftly before you saw him, of the fleeing through dark ravines, the flares dropping overhead as you ran, the deadly thrumming, percussive sound of helicopters closing in. Two minutes rest, five minutes running, nights spent in dry ravines on the West Bank. Now, in daylight, the constant danger of air raids and artillery barrages in the camps lent to the frailty of his own tent an illusion of safety, of privacy, that was almost like sleep, and he clung to it, feeling lonely and persecuted that he would have to push off with the others at dark, across into the infinite strangeness of Israel. Ashamed, he tried to think of it as the Occupied Territory, as Major Kassim always spoke of it; as his own land, in accordance with Fatah doctrine; of the raid as a homecoming. Yet it remained strangely, insistently Israel, wholly alien, as forbidding as another planet. When he thought of the Jews who tilled his father's land near Tiberias he felt nothing stronger than a deep reluctance to disturb them. His body felt drugged with fatigue; he thought desperately that he must sleep, that he would never make it tonight if he did not rest, yet he was too anxious to close his eyes. The constant movement of vehicles in the camp sent clouds of dust through the air. By the angle of sunlight at the tent opening he saw that it was already early afternoon. The anxiety he felt only increased his need for real sleep, and he would have gratefully stretched out on his cot had not the green canvas, a few inches above his head, so reminded him of the canvas shrouds of the dead.

The only means to forestall the night, he saw, was to stay awake.

Only then did Faisal admit to himself that he was frightened of the raid, as physically frightened as a boy might be of the dark, and it was a boy's fear, uncontrollable and vague, that haunted him, a fear made up of shadows and memories and the premonition of death. It was not the exhausting distance to be covered (he no

longer even thought of that), it was the almost metaphoric darkness of Israel that terrified him. He felt sure
that once across the river that night he would never return alive. This was to be his ironic homecoming. He was
as defenseless as David with his sling and stone about to
face a Goliath armed with all the cunning equipment of
the mechanized state, for the Jews had been taught by the
Germans and equipped by the Americans, and they had
learned well. Did he, Faisal Abu Ajran, really care who
owned that parched land? He had no ambitions whatever
to the farm at Tiberias, would have offered it, if it were
his, to some peasant family. For that was the whole
matter! He wanted to protest. There had been some mistake—he was a student, not a peasant! What did he care
about a parcel of earth? For him the struggle had been
joined purely out of human outrage, for the principle of
justice, not like these other, more practical, perhaps because of that less frightened men, who fought to regain a
long-remembered olive grove near Nazareth, the possession of a fruit stand in Haifa, the right, for their sons if
not for themselves, to walk once more beside the sea. He
felt infected and feverish, as if touched with the con-
tagion of Ali's distrust of the Major. For the first time
since coming to Fatah his faith was shaken. Kassim, the
Liberator, ceased to be infallible when he committed the
all-too-human error of placing Faisal in such mortal danger that he must sit thus abjectly shivering in his tent, his
shirt soaked through with sweat, cold hands folded
tightly in his lap.

You are expendable, the Major had said—Faisal remembered the very words that had elicited from Ali only
a look of contempt. *I will not die*, the Captain had said,
Not yet!

Perhaps the Captain would not, but what, Faisal wondered, of himself? He had heard older men speak of this dread, which was so like panic, though with nowhere to run. There was nothing he could do now but watch the afternoon hours wane toward evening.

The sound of an airplane, an old one, pulsed through the stillness, its reciprocating engines throbbing with antique slowness. Around him the tent walls flapped and sighed in the puffs of hot wind. A truck rumbled through the camp, rattling with tin cans, and was gone. He lowered his head into his arms and closed his eyes. But instantly he felt trapped behind the world of his eyelids, falling inward, receding helplessly farther and farther from the surface of his being, his thoughts circular and entranced in dimensionless space. Since coming to Fatah he had hardly laughed once—no one laughed—and now, with a sudden, sharp longing, he wished that he might open his eyes to find himself released from nightmare and once more in Chez Popeye, listening to the talk of the sybaritic city, watching the bright-eyed girls on Jeanne d'Arc. Even Aisa had grown somber with Fatah —had grown, somehow, old, as if he had seen too much death. Faisal dreamt uneasily of New York, of the pink sands of Jouneih, of the castles at Sidon. *We go! We go!* He snapped awake from a dream in which he seemed to hear, as if from beyond the grave, that faint and despairing voice that had cried over the radio from Deir al Quamar in that horrible recitation of fire and pain, audible across the room, to which Major Kassim had listened so impassively. Faisal awoke with a shudder. He found himself lying sprawled on his cot, still wearing his heavy boots, his back soaked with sweat, and the coffin-like wall of the canvas tent only an inch from his face.

"We go with the Captain!" the voice repeated. Faisal looked up, shielding his eyes from the light, and saw the long, civilized face of Salah grinning down at him.

"My God, I know!" he said, pulling himself up and rubbing his eyes. "Why did you have to wake me?"

"I assure you," said Salah, "that God has nothing to do with this. He isn't such a fool."

Salah, still grinning, sat down at the foot of the cot and gestured in the direction of the command post. "This is the end, isn't it?" He glanced down at the sleeping figure of Hamad. "Does he know?"

"Not yet."

"Shouldn't you tell him?"

"Let him sleep, for Christ's sake! He'll find out soon enough. I wish the Devil *I* could sleep."

Salah patted his shoulder. "Ah, the Devil—now you are invoking our true patron!"

Abruptly, Faisal felt cloaked in a gloom that was almost tangible. He was in no mood to talk to Salah, the professional optimist. Salah, born in Haifa, had been a biology teacher in the refugee camp at Wadi Sirhain, the worst sinkhole in the Amman desert, the Dachau of the Jordanian camps, where it was not the body, but the spirit, that was systematically exterminated. For eight years he had taught under UNWRA supervision, which is to say that in a small, low-roofed shed, blazing in summer and freezing in winter, he had graduated eight classes of secondary pupils, each desperate with hope for the future, only to see them sink back inevitably into the poverty and despair of the camp. The Arab states would not take them; the American Embassy granted no visas; Palestine was closed. At every turn of their lives there were signs reading "No Exit." When his first graduate was twenty-six, dead in spirit and caring only to sit in the curtained doorway of his rusting tin shack, speechless and bitter, waiting for the daily charity of the food truck, Salah, then himself only twenty-nine, left Wadi Sirhain and came to Al Fatah. But even then he came with good humor, the difference being, as he told Faisal, that the only way on this wretched earth he saw to keep his cheerful outlook on life was to get himself killed. All the rest was humbug. "If it had not been for Fatah"—he grinned—"I would have ended up in a madhouse."

"You'll end up a good deal worse tonight, if we make even one mistake," Faisal said gloomily. He was instantly sorry that he had let Salah see his mood, but now that it was too late he waited to see what impression he had made.

The grin persisted. "It's too early to worry about that. There are six hours of daylight left. Live for the day, my friend. When it begins to get dark I'll worry, too." He paused, inspecting the toes of his boots with his field knife. His voice became more circumspect. "I suppose you know what happened to Abdullah's patrol."

Faisal grunted. "They caught them in the river."

"So I heard." Salah went on, oddly constrained, without looking at Faisal. "Who was lost?"

"How should I know?" Faisal burst out with a groan. "Until I'm sitting in this tent tomorrow morning, I have better things to worry about." He took off his sweat-soaked shirt and dried his back with a towel.

Another truck went by, loaded with trenching equipment bound for Deir al Quamar, and following it was a jeep in which sat Major Kassim, looking small and insignificant next to the tall journalist, Robert Shoemaker. The sight of them, so comfortably on their way to photograph the carnage at Deir al Quamar, infuriated Faisal.

"Last night Abdullah's people blew up a pumping station and shot two Israelis," he said bitterly. "*Maybe* they shot two Israelis. And for that we have lost five men, plus the camp at Deir al Quamar, with perhaps another thirty or fifty dead." He looked at Salah levelly. "You know, I suppose, that the Major regards it a victory?"

"But of course he does, baby!" Salah replied sardonically. "He and old Braheim had it planned out from the beginning, don't you see? The Liberator and the Old Fox. Pity the Jews! There was no camp at Al Quamar. It's been a dummy blind all these months, nothing but cardboard trucks driving around, paper huts put up especially for the occasion. And those things the Jewish pilots thought were little Fatahs running for their lives? Why, those were toy soldiers. Praise God, you'd think that after all this time the Jews would have better sense! They can't outsmart Kassim! Ha, ha! Think of all the nice bombs they wasted. Do you know what a single bomb costs nowadays? And they're not rich. As I figure it, their two-plane raid on the wind-up, bleeding toys at Al Quamar, built by the wily pathans Kassim and Braheim, cost them enough to put an infantry company in the field for a year. So you see, baby, our Kassim worked it so that at the loss of only a few dozen dead (and who needs people nowadays?) we wiped out an entire company of Jewish infantry—unfortunately, also only on paper—as well as the pumping station and its two unlucky guards, who now know better, God rest their souls. What more could you ask? You can't outwit the Liberator. He says we've got more blood than they have aviation gasoline. At this rate we'll win in a year. Why, I remember once . . ."

Faisal let him talk on, without hearing the words. Salah fooled no one with his absurdity. The more he talked, the more frightened he was. It struck Faisal as worth while to note how differently they registered their fear —Salah, with his frenetic talk, he with a silent chill. If Salah would only leave him alone he could withdraw back into his thoughts; it was as if there were something waiting for him there, deep and alarming, which he had to uncover; he wanted to yawn, though he dared not sleep. Above all, he wanted to be alone. Salah, by his own choice, had become the camp clown, the butt of what bitter humor there was for the Fatah, lanky, sallow-faced Salah, the schoolteacher with the wide grin and the long legs. But he was an expert in the delicate matter of fusing plastic explosives, and a genius at disguising them. He was also a loyal fighter, one of Captain Ali's original squad, a sapper who made a brave show of believing in nothing, Fatah least of all, but could grumble cynically, "We're really in for it this time, aren't we?" and laugh at the danger, and by that gesture, with just the proper edge of heroic irony, warn you not to mistake his skepticism for cowardice. An ironist in all things, he admitted the futility, the absolute impossibility of their cause, and then, with a stoicism which only an army regular like the Captain ought to have possessed, he continued to fight— it is hopeless, you see, therefore I fight! Therefore I believe!

Yet Faisal was glad that Salah was coming along. Despite his irony (Or because of it, Faisal thought? For what was irony but an escape from ordinary, human fear?), Salah partly civilized the sinister aspect which the raid had assumed. Unable to restrain himself any longer,

Faisal interrupted his monologue to ask:

"What do you think our chances are of getting back from Beit Shal alive?"

Salah shrugged. He fell silent, his flow of words cut off in midsentence, and dug at the earth floor of the tent with his knife. Faisal, watching him consider, waiting for his answer, had a giddy sensation of falling, as if he were waiting to hear his fate pronounced. For Salah was a veteran. Like the Captain, he knew from experience what Faisal could only imagine.

"We won't have any trouble getting in," Salah said, "discounting the minor probability of a freak accident—a mine field, or a farmer out for a walk with his dog. But getting out will be another matter." He had spoken judiciously, even solemnly, giving close attention to his words; but now he grinned broadly as if to call back his own seriousness. "After that, of course, we'll be heroes! But we will be *humble*. The first thing a new hero must learn," he confided, leaning over to pat Faisal's knee, "is humility."

"If the Jews catch us, they'll drop everything they have on us." He looked up. "And who can blame them?"

"They've already dropped it on Deir al Quamar," Salah commented wryly.

"Shut up about that."

"All right, take it easy, student. How do you suppose I feel? I have friends over there."

"I'm just sick of hearing about it." Faisal looked up at the civilian face of his friend. "This won't be a reconnaissance, you know."

"Ha! I hope not! You know what I did the first time I came out of the river alone on the Israeli side? I went white funk with terror and filled my pants! All the way, as soon as I hit the West Bank! I had to crawl around like that until morning. The Jew could have found me with his nose!"

Faisal smiled in spite of himself. "Don't do it tonight."

"I wouldn't dare—not with Captain Ali. He'd cut my throat." Salah's grin faded. He regarded the tip of his knife speculatively before going on; slowly, then, he shook his head with wonder, the tension of the impending raid too much even for his cheerfulness. Remembering that first night on the dark soil of Israel, he thought of what lay ahead, waiting for them across a few hours of daylight. "Tonight," he muttered, "why *tonight*, of all godforsaken nights? After what they did to Deir al Quamar, the Jews will be on full alert. And they are *good*. They are mean bastards, but they are tough—don't think they aren't. Damn Kassim! Wouldn't any other night have done?"

Faisal imitated his irony. "Ask him."

"Ah!" Salah was sardonic. "He'd quote the training manual, number so-and-so dash such-and-such, written by fat pederasts in Beirut, lawyers and poppy addicts—forgive me, puppy, but if Fatah hadn't saved you that's what you would have been!—on the subject of the 'swift, relentless reprisals of the People's Army'!" Salah raised his hands philosophically, and with a resignation that eluded Faisal—for was this mockery, too, or the real Salah, the puny, homesick man under the hard veneer of the cynic?—he laughed and looked up at the wind-snapping ridgepole of the sweltering tent. "Well, we wanted to go home, didn't we? And we came to the right place! Yes, we did. Me, I want to see the harbor at Haifa once again before I die. Oh, that view of the orange groves from the end of the quay! Let me tell you, what a town Haifa was! On a clear day you could see halfway to Cyprus. And now Kassim, that bastard, is going to send me home in a pine box." He looked quickly down at Faisal. Purged of his bitter view of their fate, he seemed able to think once again of the raid in objective terms. Aware of Faisal's fear, he spoke in a level, reassuring tone that said, You see, I am a veteran! I know, yet I am unafraid!

"There is one thing on our side—just one. And it will bring us through, if we don't forget it."

"What's that?"

"If the Jews at Beit Shal knew we were coming, they'd be as scared as we are."

Faisal was doubtful. "Why should they be?" he asked. "Everything's on their side."

"You'll see, puppy," Salah replied enigmatically. "When we get across the river, you'll see!"

Salah left, and after a moment's hesitation—he did not want to be alone, after all, Faisal discovered; whatever was waiting for him in his inner thoughts was better left undisturbed—he leaned over to shake Hamad awake. Briefly, he told him of the raid that night against Beit Shal, that they were going as replacements with Captain Ali, and that they would get a briefing at three o'clock. Hamad took the news without any change of expression, save for a deepening gravity of consciousness in his dark eyes. "When did you say?" he asked.

"Three o'clock," Faisal repeated. Then, correcting himself, aggravated that he still could not remember the military clock: "Fifteen hundred hours, at the operations tent."

"Yes," said Hamad. "All right." He rubbed his face briskly. "How far is it to Beit Shal?"

"Fifteen miles, each way." Faisal waited to see what effect this lethal information would have on Hamad.

Hamad merely nodded objectively. "And how many hours will we have?"

"Perhaps nine."

"All right," Hamad replied. He turned over onto his side and drew his legs up, shifting his weight until the canvas cot supported him comfortably.

"What are you going to do?" Faisal asked.

"Sleep," replied Hamad reasonably, without turning his head. And then, with characteristic fatalism: "Is there anything else to do?"

When Hamad's breathing became deep and regular, Faisal left the tent, unable to bear watching him sleep, and walked down toward the command post. The camp seemed half deserted. Everyone had gone to Al Quamar. Distantly, it went through his mind that now, with Kassim, Braheim, and a hundred men trying to dig the other camp out, would be the ideal moment, the truly cunning, murderous, efficient moment for the Israelis to launch a second strike at Al Quamar. But of course it would never happen—Kassim would not die like that. Having come through so many hazards he was surely immune to anything as obvious as an air raid. No bombs would ever fall where Kassim was; and thinking this, Faisal looked quickly overhead, half expecting to see the sky full of diving Phantoms now that Kassim had removed himself, and his magical immunity, from El Husn. But the azure sky was tranquil and empty.

Faisal entered the command post still thinking of Hamad, for above everything, Hamad feared the Jewish airplanes. He feared them with an irrational, mystical fear. Men, darkness, land mines, bullets, all these were nothing

to him, compared to the incomprehensible and unfath-
omable machines, cleverly devised and treacherous,
which burst forth from an empty sky. Faisal added one
more fact to his day's education; if Salah talked, and he
suffered his incurable chill, Hamad escaped his fear of
Beit Shal, and the helicopters that would be waiting for
them at dawn, by plunging back into mindless sleep, and
he wondered if now in that sleep there were not the
whirring of rotor blades and the hollow moan of diving
jets in whatever dreams Hamad fled through.

Faisal found the radio operator carrying out the orders
Kassim had left him with—he was busy filling the air
waves with information on the intended crossing at
Mokhtara, messages to Deir al Quamar, coded relays to
Amman. He sat at a collapsible field table, his head en-
cased in a black skein of wires and earphones. The eerie,
plaintive whine of the radio signal struck Faisal's ears like
the cry of the women of Al Quamar. Picking up another
headset, he let the radio voices fill his mind, driving from
it momentarily all thoughts of the approaching night. Al
Fatah was talking from every direction of the compass;
the air strike had turned the isolated guerrilla camps from
Lebanon to Jordan into one seething matrix of anger; far
off on the slopes of Mount Barouk came the voice of Al
Fatah, promising aid to Al Quamar and vengeance to the
Jews. From the depths of the Amman desert the voice of
Fatah crackled over the blistering air, asking casualties—
this son, that brother, alive or dead?—promising futile
help, swearing implacable hatred of the enemy. An or-
chestra of hellish sounds broke forth whenever Braheim
spoke from the burned-out camp: engines, hoarse shouts,
crackling fires, drew for Faisal the scene of souls crying
out in the anguish of an inferno. If he listened closely he

heard dull thuds, secondary explosions, screams—a wail of disaster an inch from his eardrum through which, like a scene of apocalypse, he saw the stooped Kassim, long-legged Robert Shoemaker, and squat Dr. Rashid picking their way amid pieces of human wreckage. The scene was beyond reckoning, and for that very reason doubly horrible. Faisal's universe was encapsulated within the earphones; he listened with the attentive incomprehension of the blind. The command post, the waiting river, the approaching night, all were unreal. It was almost like sleep.

Slowly then, recognizing the onset of nightmare, he removed the headset and listened to the operator at the field table, afraid that if he held the earphones to his head any longer he would put his face in his arms and begin to dream. The other droned mechanically on. . . . "This is Red One calling Blue Amman Three. This is Red One calling Blue Amman Three. This is Red One calling Blue Amman Three. This is Red One calling Blue Amman Three. Do you hear me? Over." The only answering sound was the droning of a fly circling near Faisal's head. The operator began again. "This is Red One calling Blue Amman Three. This is . . ." Abruptly, he snapped the frequency to another channel, adjusted the vernier, and began again, holding his head in his hands. "This is Red One to Ahmed Four. This is Red One to Ahmed Four."

Faisal got up and went to the water cooler. He thought again of Hamad, for whom the radio was as perplexing and ominous as the enemy aircraft. Hamad had a superstitious awe of the military codes; for him they were words which no mortal could understand, a language of devils named "Blue Amman Three" and "Ahmed Four" who flew helicopters and dived down at you, machine guns blazing, out of a clear sky, devils made temporarily omnipotent by the strange, immutable will of God. It was Hamad who had said, "I will die when the Jewish pilot with blue eyes sees me near the river"; he had said it without visible emotion, merely as if stating a clairvoyant fact.

Hamad was Syrian, fully, splendidly illiterate, out of the mountains of the Jebel Druze, where, so far as Faisal knew, nothing had changed in a thousand years. Being Druze, he was an absolute fatalist. The day of his death had been ordained on the day of his birth, its manner and hour as sealed as the rising and setting of the sun. He carried a chain of glass prayer beads, its endless cycle clicking with precise regularity through his coarsened fingers, there to remind him by its clocklike fall that his time to die would come regardless of what he might do to avoid it or delay it—not an hour sooner, not one hour later. It was Hamad's faith, Faisal decided, that put him automatically out of the category of modern heroes, who suffer their fate without knowing, while for Hamad, or Hamad's God, knowing was everything. Yet the queer thing, thought Faisal, the truly perverse, human thing, was that even this blind fatalism, which should have given him a child's innocence, did nothing to quiet Hamad's mind. Hamad did not wait patiently for his death. Every day he suffered anew the terrible, gnawing sense that this day, inescapably, was *the Day*. Standing in the morning breakfast line one might see him communing deeply with himself, to stop suddenly to scan the heavens with his narrow, closely set eyes. The ominous flight of a bird, an oddly shaped cloud low on the horizon, a chance remark made within his hearing—all these were premonitory omens which he tried to read. Often he touched his wounded body, the white scar tissue made all the more conspicuous by the natural swarthiness of his skin, as if he were counting the talismans of his fate, the signs of his death which only his inner eye could read. Yet this gesture was automatic. Hamad thought little about these scars—since they had not been the scars of his death, of what importance were they?—though once, while they were digging a trench, stripped to their waists, rags tied over their heads to ward off the burning sun, Hamad had told Faisal how he came by these mementos, one night in the Negev Desert.

"I was with a patrol sent against the Kibbutz Tel Lutzal. The bedouins took us in on a caravan. The next night we mortared the compound at Tel Lutzal; then we had to cross the desert. The Jew was very angry that night. He came after us in a helicopter. Their flares dropped very slowly," he said, with reverent awe, his eyes half closed, "hung on parachutes. Beneath them the desert was as light as day. Then the helicopter gunner shot at us and flew low overhead dropping more parachutes. These were like little mushrooms, and fell quickly, but without lights. At first I didn't know what they were. Then I found out. They were little bombs, full of shrapnel, which exploded just over our heads." He pointed to a jagged, dented scar on his left shoulder. "I was running, but every time I dived into a hole, the little parachutes came down over me. They exploded everywhere, bouncing off the rocks like gravel. The Jew could move faster than we could—he hovered over us when we took cover and dropped the little bombs to drive us back into the open. When we began to run he came in behind us with his machine gun, dropping flares and letting go the little bombs again when we dived into ravines. They came down like hail, and every time one of them went off with a *bang*, the shrapnel bit like hornets. I dived into a gulley and was hit in the foot. Then I ran for a hundred yards down a sand dune and I heard the zinging noise of the metal all around me. Every time I ran I was hit. It hurt. It hurt more than I had ever been hurt in my life. Then this one hit me here"—he pointed to a white scar below his eye— "and then I got up and ran again. How I hated the Jew! He was playing with me. Then he flew away. I don't know why he did not finish me off. Maybe he was out of gasoline. All the way across the desert I was fainting from loss of blood. But of course," he concluded humbly, "it was not God's will that I die in the Negev."

In this Hamad was hardly different from the rest of them, Faisal decided, with their personal theories which, day by day, explained their survival in terms they could understand—blind fatalism, or simple luck, or theoretical, scientific statistics of hazard and probability—all alike, a set of complex and therefore totally unreliable systems. But in one thing Hamad was unique—for him there was no chance, and no hope of dumb luck, no loophole whatever. His death was fixed, the warp of Fate impenetrable. And Hamad's own particular suffering of this vision of a predestined end awaiting him had made him patient, had given him endurance and an alert, if hopeless, outlook on his life with Fatah, and a sharp eye for those clear desert skies that threatened to blow up a helicopter or a screaming Phantom out of their brooding vault to plunge him into the eternally waiting fires of Hell. All this made Faisal uneasy. Hamad's stubborn endurance was not mere human courage; if escape had been possible, Hamad, without a thought of cowardice or bravery, would have escaped. No, Hamad's endurance was rocklike and ominous, not of this world of flesh and bone and fragile hope, and thus made the world seem even more threatening and full of peril than it already was.

Faisal had met Hamad, the Druze rebel, soon after his call to Fatah had brought him out of the limbo of Beirut up to the training camp on the flanks of Mount Lebanon. At first he had felt friendless and adrift. By Fatah policy, Aisa had been taken from his side for that first week and sent to the base camp at Al Marj. At Mount Lebanon there were compulsory lectures every night to indoctrinate the recruits into the struggle and the doctrine of the new people's warfare, for if other armies marched on their stomachs, Al Fatah marched on its revolutionary spirit. It was not enough to fight; one must also think. You couldn't have men fighting to regain an orchard in Galilee until they at least understood what that orchard symbolized. The dreary outlines of these lectures were always the same, and to Faisal's educated mind they were also boringly simplistic, even childish; the open amphitheater of the hillside at night, the tense congregation of refugee youths sitting on the ground with their knees pulled tightly up under their chins in the unaccustomed chill of the high elevation, the brightly lit wooden platform with its screens and charts, the lantern slides (at which point, when the floodlights went out, Faisal dropped his head and dozed), the parade of political agents, Poles, Cubans, once even a Viet Cong, an unprepossessing little man in baggy trousers, with their maps and pointers, and their cruelly repetitive lectures, the whole scene, with its pompous exaggeration and clandestine air, so oddly pretentious for a guerrilla army that prided itself on few words but bold deeds, left Faisal feeling bored and skeptical, yet, paradoxically, only the more eager to fight.

When he took his seat on the last night, making his way amid the recruits in the dimly flickering light of a slide show, he found himself sitting next to a stocky peasant whom he recognized at once as Syrian. He was staring at the speaker with his mouth ajar, his eyes dazed with a look of total incomprehension. When the lights came on, Faisal answered his questions. What had the political agent meant by war of attrition? To Hamad, there was only one kind of war—War. Now he found that it had its slow, bleeding variety.

He thanked Faisal politely.

"It's miserably cold up here, isn't it?" Faisal said, blowing in his cupped hands, to which Hamad replied stoically, "I am from the mountains," and said nothing more.

A young Jordanian army lieutenant walked onto the stage then. He had a curious, thick British mustache, and still walked with the swagger driven into the Jordanians by their British officers during the old days of the Amman Protectorate. It had been passed on even to the younger generation of officers like himself, and now he was addressing Al Fatah recruits on the necessity of establishing bases in Jordan to break the authority of the Jordanian army and his own king, the British carry-over, Hussein. Cool, almost insolent, he explained the crimes of the Arab rulers against the refugees as one might have explained the workings of an automobile engine. He cut a clean, natty figure with his tightly buttoned tunic and his swagger stick.

"But why is he angry at the King?" Hamad whispered in bewilderment. "Is he not a Jordanian?" Faisal glanced at him suspiciously, wondering if he could really be so innocent. Momentarily, the thought crossed his mind that here perhaps was an agent planted to draw out seditious elements within the ranks of the recruits, but a few moments of conversation with Hamad cured him of the idea.

Faisal could only shake his head at the hopeless simplicity of the question, and Hamad turned back to trying to understand the significance of the movement within the refugee centers of Tripoli, Sidon, and Tyre, communication between Al Fatah and the PLO, supply from the Socialist bloc, long-range planning for a war of liberation, the inevitable joining together of the fight for Arab unification with the people's struggle against neo-colonialism in the Third World. All this was global and vast, and a perplexed dullness settled into Hamad's eyes when the speakers referred to the historical necessity, the dialectical inevitability, of Al Fatah doctrine. For what was history to Hamad? He gave up trying to fathom all this, and waited patiently, humbly, for a simple word which he could understand. When the final speaker summed up with the "dialectic of Major Arrafat," Faisal had to explain to Hamad what dialectic meant; or tried to explain, without success, as he saw when he looked at Hamad's polite, baffled eyes, which seemed to ask: Do they not know that all is fixed? That the law cannot change? That even God cannot deviate from His ordained path?

After Hamad had made the public manifesto which turned him into a hero among the recruits, Faisal had wondered how such a man had come to Fatah, instead of making a pilgrimage to Mecca. Perhaps it had been purest chance, if chance could be said to play any role in

Hamad's life. There was something so innocently obtuse
in Hamad's words that Faisal supposed he could find
himself in any situation, no matter how strange, without
the least self-consciousness. He was physically strong,
and the complete honesty and candor of his words had
issued forth like the recitation of holy writ, uncontest-
able and absolute, on the lips of an inspired illiterate. His
life had been cruel, there was that in him, too, and whatever he had endured had left an unshakable look of dignity in his eyes, like a wound which advised the world,
patiently and humbly, that he could survive any blow
that life might direct at him, and surely any blow of man,
while he awaited the final blow of God. His integrity
was beyond question, of a sort once common in Islam,
whether among bedouins, shepherds, or farmers; he was
one of the quiet, peaceful subjects of a feudal life who
could yet at certain stirring moments of history be
aroused to follow a Mohammed to conquer half the
world, or ride with Lawrence's camel corps against
Turkish machine guns. That natty, bristle-mustached
Jordanian officer, Faisal finally realized, had been
stunned into silence by the overwhelming strength of
Hamad's character, for he faced not a troublemaking student or cynic, but the very living memory of Islam, em-
barrassing, incontrovertible, and, among the recruits on
the mountain, well-nigh sacred. Thus it was that at the
end of a lecture on the political situation in the refugee
camps around Amman, and the final summing up of the
week's indoctrination which foresaw a generation of
fighting and propaganda, Hamad had risen slowly to his
feet, risen with the stubborn, unerring realization that
the week's lectures were drawing to a close and still he
did not understand. No one had yet made clear what

they wanted of him. Faisal looked up, alarmed, when he saw that his new friend was about to commit some unpardonable stupidity—saw the words taking form in his eyes, working their way to his half-opened lips, his fist rising with the slow urgency of his great need to explain himself, to comprehend the week of talk through which they had all suffered the same boredom, but at least survived. Faisal had tried to stop him, but he learned then how unacquainted he was with this taciturn, gentle peasant from Syria, for, ignoring the pull of Faisal's hand on his arm, Hamad simply raised his voice, launched it down over the heads of the entire body of recruits, rolled it down the hillside like an avalanche toward the floodlit stage, and cried out: *"I have come to die!"* A declaration? A request for clarification? Had he, perhaps, come to the wrong place? No more than that, yet the entire camp was struck dumb. In the silence that followed, the Jordanian lieutenant tapped his swagger stick in the open palm of his left hand, and peered up over the lights toward the place where that voice of rebellion or derision had come down at him. The men craned their necks to look at the author of this defiance. But Hamad stood his ground, solid and unwavering, blinking down at the lights. There had been a simple honesty in his voice that managed to keep out of his declaration any suggestion of anger or insolence. Had he looked embarrassed, or self-conscious, he would have been thrown out of Al Fatah then and there, but he stood with the innocence of a stubborn child waiting for an answer.

What answer could they give? Slowly, over the rows of heads an astonished murmur of approval welled up toward Hamad. It gained ground, swelling into a roar. "Yes," they shouted, "we have come to fight, and die!

Death to the Jews! Hurrah for Al Fatah! Long live freedom! Long live death!" And in the communal strength of that moment the Jordanian lieutenant had wisely concluded his lecture by slapping his thigh with his swagger stick and making a stiff compliment to the fighting spirit of the recruits.

From anyone else it would have been a serious offense, but no one ever spoke of it again. And to Hamad it forever remained a mystery. He had spoken the truth, and become famous. All he had wanted to know was what Fatah expected of him, what he was to understand from so much puzzling talk, to show his condition in the clearest possible way—*To die!* The political agents had harangued for a week about the people, and when they lifted their eyes in astonishment to look for the author of these simple words, the entire body of recruits recognized that there, in their midst, miraculously, stood the people.

I have come to die!

If the words had made Hamad famous, he seemed hardly to realize it. Within Fatah, both during this time and afterward, he remained contented with the lowliest of positions and the most menial of tasks. If latrines were to be dug, Hamad dug them; when they became saturated and foul, it was Hamad who filled them in and dug new ones. He hauled incredible loads on his back—81-mm shells, sacks of ferroconcrete, sandbags, coils of barbed wire and radio lead, twenty-gallon cans of gasoline. He was of an animal's endurance, and if there were those, Faisal, at first, among them, who were disappointed to find that in this gleaming example of the common man there was nothing which could be stirred to a higher awareness, Hamad himself was supremely unaware that he had either amazed or disappointed anyone. At times he would sit on his cot in the tent which he shared with Faisal, Aisa, and two other fighters, meditating profoundly, while in his speechless way he ticked the glass beads of his rosary through his fingers, the endless cycle forming in his mind (so Faisal guessed) a litany of the repetition of time, of the sameness of all things, their common fate, regeneration, and infinite deaths. The sun rose; the sun set; the planets and stars wheeled through their ancient courses; and at the center of it all Hamad waited. Faisal watched, fascinated, while Hamad studied the flight of evening swallows, flitting upward only to tumble down invisible shafts of air, swooping and darting like bats, and he wondered what went through that mind that seemed to have for its one subject the history, the reverses, the bewilderments, wanderings, and the final death of Hamad, the Son of Hamad.

For underneath that taciturn mask, at the very ground of his being, Faisal finally came to understand, Hamad— like all of them—was cursed with an intellect lively enough to imagine, and so suffer in advance, every conceivable form of death. Born into the Jebel Druze, into that wild and desolate place, even Hamad (so Faisal sensed) felt himself cut off from man and God, and trapped like all of them in a predicament from which there was only one mode of exit, and that a greater mystery than all the rest. Of his life in Syria he seldom spoke, barely enough to allow Faisal to see into his thoughts, where there ran a constant film of Hamad's life, being watched, day and night, by Hamad. The man, Faisal thought, was almost insane with this preoccupation with his own destiny—or would have been judged insane in the West, where, stripped of his Druze faith, no doubt he

would have seemed so to himself. As a young man he had
been married to the daughter of an even poorer peasant,
and in those Syrian mountains, snowbound half the year
—where the Druze had withdrawn centuries before to
suck the dry bone of their faith, and where it existed in
its pristine fanaticism alone down to the present—Hamad
tilled the rocky slopes as the tenant of a feudal sheik,
Sa'id Bek. Within a few years he had an infant son and a
sickly, tubercular wife to keep warm, to feed, and somehow to clothe; the sheik took three fourths of the crop,
and Hamad kissed his hand. At night his diseased wife
huddled in a corner of their stone hut, using her body's
warmth to keep the child alive. The stones were not
mortared, and the wind cut through the cracks like a
knife. Hamad, alone, slept in another corner, waiting.
Then one day, when the brutality of his life had become
unbearable, he returned home to find his wife's family
wailing and tearing their hair outside the hut; the wife
was dead, the child dying. When the sheik came Hamad
struck him in the face. He thought he might have killed
him; he never found out, for he ran away before the
sheik's family murdered him. He made his way to the
slums of Damascus, meditating all the way, two weeks of
walking at night through deserts and farms, on the
strange fate that was sending Hamad, the Son of Hamad,
so unexpectedly away from his home. In Damascus he
first worked as a porter, hauling tremendous loads across
the markets on leather straps bound to his forehead and
shoulders. He accepted whatever came his way, slept in
gutters when there was no work, ate to surfeit when he
could against the days when he could not, forever standing back from himself, observing the working out of that
fate which was drawing him on. His life had become a

puzzle to him, which only the loss of his life could solve
—to know the final answer, the place and time of it, the
manner of dying, to see the whole plan finally carried
out, each piece in its proper order, became an obsession.
He watched with the avidity of a child being told a
story, one of those interminable Arabic tales which wind
and twist through a labyrinth of causality and at last finish with some unexpected absurdity. He had come to
Fatah because one day in the worst alleys of Damascus,
where people went hungry in the streets and the children
begged, and only the strong, like Hamad, could make
enough to survive, he was approached by a man who
took him to a political meeting. When it was over, he had
volunteered for Fatah, and all the while, inwardly, the
real Hamad was watching the agent with fascination,
wondering, *Is this the man?* and following his every suggestion as if it had been an edict of God—which, indeed,
to Hamad it was. It was not that he was a fool. He realized perfectly well that this agent was only a man, that
he knew nothing of the immensely important fate being
so diligently spun around Hamad Abu Hamad, the Son
of Hamad. That was his one conscious superiority, that
he alone knew the secret use to which these people were
being put who so unexpectedly entered upon the stream
of his life, to bend it in the direction it must inevitably
go—Sa'id Bek, the agent in Damascus, the Jordanian officer on faraway Mount Lebanon. They were the conduc-
tors of his fate, sent to convey him, at last, to the rendezvous which had been waiting in the cold, wheeling stars
since the day of his birth, since the creation of the planets, out of time unimaginable. And now, thought Faisal,
he, too, kicking Hamad's cot to wake him up, informing
him of the raid that night against Beit Shal, he, too, had

taken his place in Hamad's pantheon of demigods sent, all unknown to themselves, to play the role of Dark Angel.

It amused Faisal, and it also irritated him. Most of all, perhaps, it made him envious, for of all the men he had ever known Hamad was the only one who would, at his death, be able to sigh with final release, "At last, *at last!*" Hamad was mad, and sitting over the table in the command post Faisal thought that he could use a little of that madness himself to calm the uprooted, lonely feeling of hanging drunkenly above an abyss, blood rushing in his ears, clutching in terror at the substanceless hours which ticked away the afternoon.

At three o'clock on that blazing hot afternoon of August 6, Faisal, Salah, and Hamad were standing before the map table in the operations tent. Ali folded back the tent flap to let in a flood of golden sunlight, and took a map down from the rack behind him. They all bent over the map, where Ali marked with a blue pencil.

"The target the Major has assigned us is the electrical generating station, here, at Beit Shal." He looked up at them. "I have decided that the Major is wrong; the generating plant is too heavily defended. Instead, we will attack the towers on the hill behind the station. Do any of you object?" He looked at them for a moment longer; then, nodding, he turned to the wall map. "All right, we will cross three miles above Mokhtara. Our people will make a diversionary attack on the outposts, there, to draw the enemy down the river. Fifteen minutes later, we cross, two at a time, five minutes apart. We will take the route away from Kibbutz Steinmetz, here, and move through Jezzine, to a point, there, twelve miles into enemy territory. You, Salah—pay particular attention.

There is a bridge there across a ravine which you will mine going in. I want exactly three hours to reach Beit Shal from the bridge and get back. Set your timers precisely. There will be no chance to mine anything on the way out. We will cross the bridge ten minutes before it blows up. That will cut the road from Beit Shal, and slow down their pursuit. From the bridge we leave the road and return by way of Jezzine." He was silent for a moment. "Are there any questions?" No one spoke. The Captain leaned back against the table and looked at them levelly. "Surely you have questions. Let me hear them. We must consider every possibility."

Faisal struggled to formulate something; time seemed to have unspooled past him in a great spiral, and for an instant—his mind still grappling with the shocking fact that so much of the day was already lost, that they were standing in the Captain's tent, three hours from dusk—for an instant he went blank. He wondered if this would happen to him when the crisis came across the river. He forced himself to speak.

"What time will we reach the bridge?" he asked.

"Before midnight, if we are not delayed by patrols."

"And when do the mines go off at Beit Shal?"

"If Salah does his work properly," said Ali, throwing him a stern look, "they will go off at precisely fifteen minutes after the bridge—at 0215, when we will be off the road and down in the valley. By the time the Jews reach the cut bridge, I estimate that we will have gotten halfway to the Jordan. That will leave us seven miles to go after the mines explode, and the chase begins."

"Let me see the target again," Salah said.

The Captain pulled out another, more detailed map. "There it is," he said reflectively. "The Jews are very proud of it. They have just built it. They're putting up permanent installations like that everywhere in the West Bank, to prove that they are determined to keep the territory they gained in 1967. It's too big to destroy, but if we take out the towers here, where they go over the hill behind the station, we will make what the Major wants—a bang they will hear all the way to Tel Aviv." Ali was silent for a moment, letting them study the map, letting them think what, for the Jew, it would be like to have the hand of Fatah reach into their homes and snap out the lights. That silent, vigilant warning would be more frightening than a hundred air raids, would weigh more heavily on Jewish minds than an infantry division across the border. "Don't believe what you hear about the Jew," Ali said. "He is tough, as I know from experience, and even without his mechanized equipment, he is good. You cannot break his will. But he is a sentimentalist; you can break his heart. And that is just what we want to do—break his heart. Make him give up the fight. When he spends a few nights in a dark house, with a candle on a plate, and his women and children around him, he will realize that he can never be secure on the West Bank. The Jews are fond of their children."

Salah shoved his hands into his pockets. "How much plastic can you give me?"

"How much can Hamad carry?"

"Fifty pounds," Hamad said unhesitatingly.

"No, not running fifteen miles, you idiot! I'll give him twenty-five," the Captain said, turning back to Salah, "and the rest of us will take fifteen pounds of plastic, along with our other equipment. If we are going to travel fast, we must stay light."

"Seventy pounds of plastic," said Salah, pursing his lips

contemplatively. "That's a lot—if we don't lose any."

"Not going in," said Ali. "And coming out, there'd better not be any left to lose."

"How many towers do we mine?"

"Four."

Salah's face grew more interested as he studied the map of Beit Shal. In the enlargement, streets, houses, and underground pipes were clearly marked. "This is their garrison, here?"

"Yes. We think it's only a company of local militia, no regular troops. We're counting on that. We'd never get through the security pickets of a main line unit. They may have police dogs. We can't be sure. The local Palestinians are under curfew in that area, so our intelligence is unreliable."

"Then," said Salah, "they will come down this stretch of road first, out of Beit Shal, before turning east."

Ali made a general sweep of his hand over the map to indicate the uncertainty of pursuit. "They will come across that road, yes, unless they fan out north and south, leaving it to the river patrols to block the area between Beit Shal and the Jordan. One factor that might make them hesitate to move eastward at once is that, striking that deep, they might think we won't try to recross the river but will look for sanctuary in an Arab village somewhere on the West Bank."

"Still," Salah persisted, "some troops will come down that road as soon as the mines go off."

"What are you driving at?"

"Just this. We could give them a nice little surprise by setting a mine on this stretch. There is a drainage tunnel marked on the map, under the road. It should be possible to blow that up with a contact mine."

The Captain was dubious. "It will take you too long to plant an extra charge, and we won't have time to waste."

But Salah was growing visibly attached to the idea of mining the culvert road. "Faisal can do the drainage tunnel while we do the towers." Salah winked at Faisal. "You want to give them a surprise, Captain. Shake them up a little, not just one bang and then run for our lives. A left, a right, then a left! Knock them around a bit. Make them break out the mine detectors, and step gingerly. The beauty of plastics is all in the surprise. Reach for a doorknob, and *bam!* it blows your arm off. One blast, then another, then when they're still off balance, coming down that road like the Devil, *boom!* another. It's a question, you see, of aesthetics."

Ali glanced doubtfully at Faisal. "Are you capable of setting a C-4? We'll have only a few minutes to spare. It won't do us any good if you blow yourself up in that drainage pipe."

Salah laughed. "Mines, plastics, booby traps—oh, yes, he can do it all! No doubt about that." He grinned at Faisal. "Whether he wants to do it or not is another matter."

"I will do it," Faisal answered.

"All right," Ali said, "if we can hit them a third time, I am for it. But I want Faisal with us on the hill; he'll cover us while we set the charges on the towers. Let Hamad mine the road. He'll carry the C-4 and detonators. The usual precautions apply—face grease, no metal parts touching, nothing reflective, bring your camouflage netting."

Hamad, who had started visibly when he heard that he was to mine the culvert, looked up.

"But we won't need the nets," he said, "unless we are

caught by sunrise—"

"In which event," Ali replied flatly, "we will need them very much. If we don't reach the river by dawn," he said, "we separate. From then on it's every man for himself. Find a hole and stay under your netting until dark."

There was a moment of silence in the tent, during which they all fixed their eyes on the map. It was Faisal who spoke.

"Tell me, Captain," he asked, "what would you do if you had to spend tomorrow behind enemy lines?"

"If I lost my temper," said Ali truthfully, "I would shoot it out, and die. If not, and the Jews found me, I would surrender. For yourselves, I advise you to surrender if you are trapped. There is no disgrace in that— not when you are alone."

Faisal looked at him closely. Was that why he wanted them to separate in case of trouble, so that each of them, unknown to the others, could surrender in good conscience rather than be drawn into the futility of a last fight? The Captain had not surrendered on Hill 203; but then, Faisal remembered, that had been in full view of embattled Jerusalem, the second city of Islam, in the eye of the world and at a moment, at least for the Captain, of near triumph. Was it different now that the Captain was a guerrilla? Perhaps this was what Kassim had failed to take into account, that once across the Jordan at night the Captain would be alone, without an audience, answerable only to himself. Would he surrender to the Jewish regulars?

"Whatever else he may be," Ali said, "the Jew is not a criminal. He will not execute you. Prison would not be easy to endure, but remember that a settlement could one day come that would liberate you. My advice is: if you are caught tomorrow morning west of the Jordan, with no chance of crossing, give yourselves up." He looked at all of them. "If there are no other questions I will see you here at 1700, fully equipped."

When they had left the tent Faisal turned to Salah. "What about you, Salah? What would you do? I mean, if the Jews trapped you."

Salah grinned, glanced up at the sky, then at Hamad, who walked beside them. The teacher's eyes lit with a peculiar gentleness. "There is no need for any more of us to die than must," he said. "We lost five men last night; I don't care to be among the four who die tonight."

Faisal persisted. "Then you would surrender?"

Salah's smile was enigmatical. "Maybe."

Faisal thought again of Captain Ali, whom they had left in the operations tent, staring at the map as if hoping to gain some last-minute clue to the imponderables which awaited them across the river. Faisal was still caught in the uncanny feeling that it could not be so late, already four o'clock, the sky beginning to pale toward evening. He had the sensation of febrile alertness that comes from days of sleeplessness, a brittle, glasslike clarity of vision which rendered everything unreal, as if he were viewing it through the wrong end of a telescope. "How about you, Hamad?" he asked, blinking upward at the sky.

"*Hamdullah*," replied Hamad indifferently. "Thanks be to Allah, I am always ready to die."

A truck moved through the open camp in a cloud of dust. Faisal bade his friends goodbye, and turned toward his tent, determined to lie down and close his eyes; if he could not sleep, he would force himself to rest quietly until it was time to assemble his gear. The evening wind was springing up as the blanket of heat began to rise off the earth, kicking up sand devils that trailed across the hillside. Salah turned down toward the command post, when he saw Major Kassim and Robert Shoemaker striding toward them.

"Faisal," the Major said, "please go to the truck where the bodies of Abdullah's people are waiting. I am sorry, but there is something you must do there. Mr. Shoemaker will accompany you." His voice was brisk and matter-of-fact; he strode away with short, choppy steps, his loosely fitting dungarees flapping in the wind.

The truck from Golan was covered with dust, and in the hot wind the canvas tarpaulins over the three bodies snapped stiffly like sailcloth. The two men from the Golan camp, back to their work after the interruption of the raid on Deir al Quamar, sat on the running board of the truck, making out identification tags to tie to the feet of the dead. They had not yet uncovered their faces— now they did so. When the green canvas was pulled back to disclose the face of the second body Faisal felt as if his heart had stopped. The eyes of the dead fighter were partly open, as if with a final thought, as if, in his plunge earthward, he had tried to speak a final word. Frozen, he tried to speak it still. As Faisal bent nearer that face the breeze lifted a lock of hair, let it fall back, lifted it again. Around his dark, curly hair pieces of grass clung, matted, as if in his last fall to earth he had splashed into shallow water. Beneath the clear brow and the speechless, thoughtful eyes, the throat had been blown out of sight. Reluctantly, Robert Shoemaker stepped back to take a photograph.

The dead fighter was Aisa.

A Death

IN a concealed ravine a hundred yards from the banks of the Jordan, the four-man squad of Al Fatah, their faces blackened with charcoal and grease, waited in the deepening twilight for the signal to move out. Salah was adjusting for the last time the straps of Faisal's pack. "It was miserable luck," he said quietly, "for Aisa to die like that." The ravine ran at a transverse angle to the river-bank, where Captain Ali was watching the west shore through binoculars. He turned his head sharply.

"Be quiet," he ordered.

The diversionary group was ready to strike at Mokh-tara. When they began to hear the distant rattle of small-arms fire they knew they had just fifteen minutes more to wait before the first two, the Captain and Salah, pro-tected by the sudden fall of dark, attempted the crossing. Faisal inspected the seals on Hamad's packs of explosives, then Salah's. Everything was ready. He peered nervously toward the low, flat shadow of the river, already dissolving into night. Faint stars flickered in the pale dusk, though evening had brought no relief from the day's smoldering heat. It lay over the riverbank still, damp and stifling, enwrapping them like a shroud. Behind him Salah was picking absently at the palm of his hand with the point of his field knife. "It was so stupid to die like that," he said. "He wasn't even supposed to be in Abdullah's group."

"Shut up about it, can't you? It doesn't matter what we think," Faisal added flatly, still staring at the ominous shadow of the river. "He is dead. There is nothing we can do."

Salah glanced warily at him for a moment, then drew his lean height down into a compact ball, his head two feet below the crest of the ravine, closed his eyes, and fell silent. Faisal remembered the hand of Robert Shoemaker on his shoulder—"I am sorry," the American had said, but still he had stepped back and snapped the picture, eminently newsworthy, of Faisal kneeling beside the body of his friend. Faisal had lunged at him then; he had snatched the miniature camera from the journalist's hands and ground it to bits under his boot. Then he had waited, helplessly, for whatever madness was rising up within him to take possession of his soul. But the upheaval did not come; it remained half-flowered, like some monstrous, stillborn, hellish wail of grief in a depth of his being that he had never felt before, it lay in his insides with a sickening, insulting impact, like the blow of a fist in his stomach. That howl of grief was coiled in his guts now, and he knew that he would never get it out. Whenever he thought of Aisa's half-opened eyes, trying to speak to him, of the throat torn away, he felt himself driven from remote abstraction to sudden outbursts of violent anger. He remembered once, in what seemed now like another world, having taken a book off a dusty shelf in the university library (it was the unlikely title that had attracted his eye, gold embossed on rich leather, *Restorative Surgery of War Wounds*); he remembered standing in the mellow, golden light of a tall window, idly turning the pages, coldly fascinated—colored plates of men with black, triangular holes where once had been noses, the unique wedges of cartilage clipped by shell fragments as neatly as by a scalpel; men with their entire lower jaw shot away, the upper teeth protruding, canine, into nothingness; men with empty eye sockets and throats reduced to cords of twisted purple scar tissue. Aisa's face had been like that. Faisal tried to drive away the image, but soon his own lower jaw began to ache in obscene, uncontrollable mimicry of his friend; his straining heart beat painfully in every part of his body, but nowhere as laboriously as through the great arteries of his throat, where Aisa had received his death wound. His mood had become vague and unpredictable even to himself. Still half dazed, he was subject to shift from bitter, wordless grief to violent accusation without the least warning. He felt inwardly murderous. Salah had never known him so short-tempered before, only to fall at once into a profound and brooding meditation. As they had walked to the truck that was to drive them to their jumping-off point, he had hardly dared to say a word, except to observe, pointlessly, for the dozenth time, that it had been rotten luck.

"Why didn't you stay off the patrol tonight?" he had asked. "You're in no shape to go to Beit Shal. Tell Ali you're sick."

To which Faisal had answered with such explosive

wrath that Salah felt as if whole layers of flesh had been flayed from his body.

Now the Captain shifted his weight the better to hear the mounting pitch of the distant fire fight. "Listen," he said. "They are crossing at Mokhtara."

Soon they could hear mortars added to the dull knock of rifles. The solid, nerve-jarring crump of the 81-mm shells fell with the regularity of a mechanical hammer. Someone was laying down a walking barrage, probing for his opponent's hiding place, though whether it was on their own or the Jew's side of the river they could not tell. In the growing darkness a preliminary flare rose, ignited brilliantly, and slowly drifted back to earth.

"They're trying to keep them off the river."

"That's Kassim for you," murmured Salah. "He'll get half a dozen men shot up just to put us across onto the West Bank. And he'll have us ground to pieces by dawn to blow out the lights at Beit Shal. How he must hate the Jews!" He added, glancing at Faisal, "Don't worry though, to hell with Kassim! We'll blow those towers up anyway, only for ourselves, and for Aisa, not for him."

The gunfire below on the river made Faisal fretfully alert once more. His blood prickled with impatience. "I wish they'd get it over with!" he whispered vehemently. "We could have been across five times by now, even in daylight."

Ali turned to look at him, but said nothing. Faisal, in his urgency to begin, to flee that death mask which seemed to wait with them in the ravine, crept forward to where the Captain was watching the far bank. Crouching beside Ali quieted his nerves, as if there, by merely sharing his close attention to the first details of the raid, he was no longer passively awaiting his fate.

The Captain's appearance, despite the irregular outfit of the guerrilla, managed somehow to preserve an aspect of military severity. The camouflage jump suit, the web belts, the black knit skullcap could not hide the disciplined, methodical hardness of the infantry officer beneath. At his side he wore a .45 automatic in a leather holster, dulled to prevent its reflecting light. The heavy, cannonlike weapon, thought Faisal, summed up the Captain. It was not Fatah equipment, but regular Jordanian army issue, American-made, as useless in night combat as a club, yet as much a part of the Captain's harness as the swagger sticks, shoulder grenades, and ivory-handled revolvers which officers in every army affected in their quizzical, almost paranoid regard for their own dignity. The .45 was the last remnant of Ali's army life, the sign of his limited, personal rebellion. It belonged as much as the sobriquet, *Al Sakhr*, the Rock, belonged, for they were emblems of a mute, stolid resistance both to the Jews and Al Fatah alike.

Faisal could no longer see the river. A moonless night had fallen with desert suddenness, leaving everything around them as dark as the bottom of a well. Overhead there were only the faint pinpoints of the first stars. He felt Hamad move closer in the darkness, and heard a faint, careless jingle of metallic equipment. "Tighten up!" he whispered furiously, and turned Hamad roughly around to find the source of that delicate, glasslike sound which, magnified in his overly tensed state of mind, he saw causing all their deaths at some imagined, cinematic moment in the hours that lay ahead. Down the river the Israeli flares continued to go up—one, two, three, in regular order. Nothing could live on the river in such illumination. The Israeli patrols from the sector opposite them would, hopefully, be closing on Mokhtara. But could they really be so easily deceived as that? he wondered.

"They're overdoing it," Ali muttered.

Salah moved up behind them. "Yes, the Jew is not such a fool, is he?"

Ali cursed between his teeth, and moved farther away, toward the invisible point where the ravine turned to face the riverbank, and down which they would have to file, one by one, when it came time to cross. For a moment of absurd, furious panic, Faisal wondered if the Captain was leaving them, if he would crawl off into the night to some hidden safety he had prepared for himself, to let them live or die by their own wits.

A heavy machine gun had opened up south at Mokhtara. The sound of it, dull and emphatic against the shrill, impatient chatter of lighter weapons, made Faisal think of bullets the size of fists slamming into the mudbanks. He envied the machine gunner. It would have relieved his own pent-up feelings to have snapped his Sten gun off his shoulder and sprayed the opposite bank of the river, to see the angry, red tracers flashing across to snuff themselves out in darkness.

"There," Salah whispered, "one of ours."

Faisal grunted, assenting impatiently to the obvious, and moved away. Now that the Captain had left them to listen along the riverbank, Faisal again had the giddy sensation of having been abandoned in a dark place. The night pressed against his face, as thick as felt; he wanted to wipe something away from before his eyes, as if the veil of darkness were tangible, clinging to him with the horror of a spider's web. In a half-stupor he fumbled over his harness, checking what he had already checked countless times, muttering with frustration—buckles, straps, the equipment in his waterproofed leg pockets, the safety of his Sten gun, the long, deadly, oiled clips of ammunition across his chest. Ahead, on the riverbank, frogs—Kassim's favorite image of the Jew—had begun a hollow croaking; their noise filled Faisal with an inhuman, cold despair, so perfectly suited were they to his mood of stupefied wonder. The sound was almost more than he could bear. An insect crawled over his hand; the flares went up at Mokhtara; the frogs' brainless song continued; the damp heat clung to him. Aisa's death had made him want to kill, to liberate savagely that reptilian wail of anguish that still lay coiled in his stomach. The sight of his friend's face had set off something within him; the thought, or something below thought, a deep indwelling awareness of all that was alien that had tried to rise to consciousness while he waited in his tent, now occupied the center of his mind. He had been taught that the word "nothing" had no significance, that there was no such category in the mind, but now he knew that there *was* such a category, an empty place which he had never known before, but which had been suddenly thrown open and threatened to extinguish all else. And there was a word that corresponded to this awareness of nothingness, which sprang from it—the word was "dread." He felt all this again when the Captain left; it was not only dread of the dark, or the pain and shock of death, nor even the horror, quite, which had frozen him with that sunlit vision of Aisa's wasted face (for he could not think of his friend now; that face was no longer human, it was "other," like the frogs' brainless chorale, the insects, and the darkness of the ravine, and filled him with a cold revulsion), but, rather, a deeper anger, a rage of helplessness that held them all in bondage, a cool, insolent voice that told them that their puny freedom was at an end. They were in its hands now, subject to one law: Kill, or be killed! How could he have forgotten what this blind rage was like? For it was this way each time he came to the Jordan at night, to cross for a hundred yards and return, no less than for this deep raid against Beit Shal, with a return—when? How could anyone say? Would they ever return at all? It was Kassim's voice which had exploded their personal ideas of Fatah. You will kill or be killed! the Major said—you are, above all, *expendable*. And it was the Major, not just Aisa, who waited with them now in the ravine, and it would be only the Major who awaited them when they returned. That was what he had meant by electrical generating stations, and a bridge at Beit Shal—his own authority. They had submitted themselves to it, each for his own reasons, and were as helpless now as slaves. Whatever belief had brought them to that dark riverbank, strapped under the deadly weight of *plastiques* and Sten guns and webs of ammunition, their motives had been violated beyond recognition. For months they had slept through their training like cataleptics, still moving in a dream world where one fought on his own terms, only to awaken in horror to find that, after all, they had only been brought to the East Bank of the Jordan, facing a night in which, like all those who had gone before them, they would respond to nothing more humane or dignified than the dark, barbaric instinct of survival. They would kill, Faisal thought, not for Al Fatah, not for the people or any idea of justice, perhaps not even to avenge Aisa, but merely to stay alive. Merely out of fear. He felt restless and bitterly tired and humiliated. Faisal wondered if Aisa had been afraid the night before, as he knew that Salah was afraid now. Even the Captain, for all his methodical preparations, must surely know this fear—resentment, disgust at their personal helplessness—despite the fact that his fear was covered with a stubborn, military pride.

Perhaps of them all, thought Faisal, only Hamad, with his Druze fatalism, remained unafraid of that otherness of death, that dread of empty things. Or was this cold fear, this prevision of disaster, precisely what Hamad suffered every waking hour of his miserable life? With a shudder, Faisal closed his eyes, praying that when he opened them again it would be time to start.

"We are going to come out, Faisal, you and I," Salah whispered, crouching behind him. "You and I are going to make it back. We are coming back if we have to fly!" There was a tone in his voice that Faisal had never heard before, a hard core of rebellion at Kassim and all that lay behind them, forcing them on, and at the Jew who surely lay in wait for them somewhere ahead. Salah was concerned with neither killing nor dying. His irony was gone. He would fuse his lovely plastics and return.

Faisal said nothing. Ali had come up the ravine. Suddenly Faisal felt his presence close by in the darkness. For a brief second he saw the flash of his luminous wrist watch. The Captain's flat voice broke the silence, startlingly close by.

"It is time. Salah will come with me. You and Hamad wait five minutes. If nothing happens, follow. We will hear you."

The Captain's final words, that no matter how cautious they were, their crossing through the shallow sandbanks of the river could be heard by anyone listening on the West Bank, tightened Faisal's nerves to a final pitch.

He wanted to make some appropriate reply, but could think of nothing before the Captain and Salah disappeared. In the ravine there was a terrible, lonely difference when the two were gone. For the last time, he and Hamad tightened the straps of one another's packs. Hamad slid the bolt of his Sten gun back, with a sharp click. "Quiet!" snapped Faisal, while ahead of them, not all at once, but gradually, his inner sense piercing the thick darkness, he became aware of Ali's and Salah's position in the water. He could not see them, but he could feel them, two points which in all the empty night were not empty, but mysteriously vibrant with life, moving away. With an animal's sense for living things, he felt them reach the far shore, where his acute perception of them dissipated away into the general blackness and strangeness of everything that lay beyond the river. It was as if they had been swallowed up in the maw of darkness. The blackness where the river was, and where he and Hamad would have to go, was again merely empty. When they had waited long enough, he touched Hamad's arm.

"Now," he said. "Keep close."

"I'll be two feet behind you," replied Hamad.

Moving down the open mouth of the ravine, reaching the first, treacherous softness of the muddy bank, Faisal felt as if they were edging blindly toward a precipice. But the riverbed flattened out and silently, swinging his legs forward without splashing, he began to wade. With no visible distinction between the water, the air, the shore they had left, Faisal at first felt smothered and a little panicky. When the water was up to his waist, wading with his gun over his head, he had to fight down a momentary, urgent need to suck in a deep breath—for if he allowed himself to inhale, he knew, it would come out a hoarse shout. There was a quality of desperation, too, in Hamad's dogged silence behind him. Faisal, edging forward through the current, testing the footing with each step, afraid, more for his sanity than the equipment, of stepping into a hole in the sandy bottom and going under—once in that total blackness, swept by the current, how could anyone find his way back to the surface? you would drown thrashing in four feet of water—heard the strained breathing of Hamad at his back; he was wheezing through his clenched teeth, as if the water were freezing, though it was disgustingly, swampishly warm. He was making too much noise, splashing with his shorter, thicker body, and it alarmed Faisal, who wanted to caution him; but he knew that if he stopped now Hamad would collide with him, and it would be impossible not to be heard. Even if they remained silent, he thought, feeling a sudden, deep chill, as if cold, unfriendly eyes were watching them from the other bank, could not their exact position be sensed, as he had sensed the Captain and Salah crossing? What if a flare went up now? There would be just time to look overhead, mouth agape in stupefied wonder, before the inevitable burst of machine gun fire knocked you over backward into the river. Faisal shivered involuntarily, but now the water was down to his knees; he was moving faster, slodging up out of the mudbank, doubled over, almost running, with the dripping, shambling sounds of Hamad coming at his heels. When they reached hard earth Faisal dropped down on one knee, his eyes straining to pick out the Captain in the dark, and waited. For a moment there was total silence; then, with a jolt, as if his eyes had suddenly opened, Faisal felt the Captain's presence a few feet from them. Faisal's heart was pounding wildly. But there was no trace of emotion in Ali's voice as he turned away, exposed the dial of his wrist watch for a brief second, and said:

"We have two hours until moonrise. Stay close, and keep quiet."

The four started out without delay. A vehicle, its headlights probing the dark like the twin antenna of a night insect, was moving at right angles to them on the first Israeli road, perhaps a troop carrier, or an ambulance, on its way to the fight at Mokhtara. When it had passed they crossed the road without event, one at a time, plunging down at once into the darkness of open fields. Ali set a pace which would bring them out at the bridge in two hours, and to Beit Shal in three. Faisal fell in with a low-hipped, athletic stride, moving methodically, holding back his strength, head down and slightly forward, arms bent at the elbows against the weight of his pack. For the first half mile the country continued flat; then, climbing steeply between boulders, Ali led them across the flank of a low hill. Beneath them Faisal could make out the deeper black of a ravine, running off to the south; it was this that Ali had avoided. A few scrub pines rose above them on the spine of the hill, silhouetted against the faint stars, the night's heat drawing the pungent sap from their bark. They crossed a goat path, then descended. Again the terrain leveled off. The Captain, turning left, led them down into the cover of a shallow gulley.

Faisal was astonished at the pace the Captain was setting. It was the forced march of the infantryman, determined, unhesitant, closer to a run than a walk. Faisal had thought that even *Al Sakhr* would have to slow down when they left the banks of the Jordan, but the remorseless pace did not slacken. If anything, it increased. Faisal soon found himself winded. His clothing was quickly soaked; beads of sweat stood out on his forehead, gathered maddeningly over his eyes, ran across his open lips, touching them with brine, trailed in rivulets down his sides and back. Shifting the weight of his pack, he wiped his right arm across his forehead, but his sleeve, already soaked through with sweat, only smeared the blackening and grease on his face. He gave up and tried to ignore the discomfort, though soon he felt as if flies were crawling over his eyelids. The suffocating, dusty, black heat of Israel enwrapped them like a shroud. He heard Hamad gasping behind him. Ahead Salah was wheezing audibly. As they stumbled through the darkness it seemed to Faisal that they all made enough noise to be heard for a mile. He looked up frequently, expecting to see the muzzle flashes of a Jewish machine gun lying in carefully prepared ambush, the tracers gliding toward them, to snap by instantly past their heads, the long, dark plunge earthward, perhaps, with a bullet in one's face.

Yet nothing disturbed the progress of their march. The dry ravines down which Ali led them were strewn with boulders and soft, treacherous pockets of sand. Salah went down, got up cursing, and lunged on. Faisal wondered what the Captain would do if he tripped and broke an ankle. Would Ali leave him behind? He knew the answer: Ali would leave him.

Each time they came over a hill and descended into the sloping bottom of the ravines where the heat lay in wells, Faisal felt himself going down into it as if he were sliding under water. Often, crossing open fields, they saw lights to the north. These, Faisal knew, remembering the operations map, were the fortified Jewish settlements of the

Bikhazi. The Captain gave them a wide berth. Of the two patrols sent against them in the last month, not a man had survived. When the squad found themselves in open ground they broke into a flat run, doubled over, as if they were still running through the infantry course on Mount Lebanon with the training officers cursing them over loudspeakers. As often as they crossed one ridge of stony hills another rose up ahead of them, indistinct shadows blocking their path like natural sentinels, which became an ordeal of boulders, crevices large enough to swallow a man's foot, and gravel moraines over which they had to drag themselves, gasping with exertion. Ali, as sure of his direction as a ferret, plunged downward through the dry wadis, always finding a sheltered gulley where he slowed to a fast walk, twisting his way unerringly between rocks and brittle copses of dwarfed trees.

Yet if Faisal's body groaned with the cruel rhythm of the march, his spirit grew lighter. He saw that he had exaggerated the danger of the raid. Already he was deeper into Israel than he had ever been before, and though he felt all the familiar, nearly physical hostility that emanated from this ground so long held by the enemy, his fear diminished. The Captain's pace was brutal, but he was young, he could stand it. What amazed Faisal was that, while every step forward ought to have slammed steel doors behind them, they had come unharmed through open fields and narrow, easily watched ravines, perfect for ambush, where the wary Jew, if he was going to stop them, should have stopped them. So it was not so difficult, Faisal concluded with grim satisfaction, to take a night walk into Israel. The Jew was vulnerable after all. For all his mighty armament he could not secure the doors of his own house. With bitter pleasure, he admitted the truth of Kassim's dictum: The Jews had swallowed more land than they could control. They were short of men, stretched on their bloated frontiers from Syria to the Suez; everyone knew that. They guarded the farms and irrigation canals and the approaches to the towns, but they had to trust to luck with the rest. And tonight, Faisal thought vengefully, the memory of Aisa's brutally shattered face burning in his mind, tonight their luck was going to be bad.

Faisal could not drive away that smoldering memory. The face hung before him as if it were barely two feet in front of his eyes, slightly higher than his line of vision, an evil, illuminated Saint Christopher preceding him into the darkness of Israel. Again he saw the dead eyes, the lower jaw half carried away, the clotted remnants of the throat so cruelly mangled by the shell that had killed him. Why Aisa? What had Aisa done to merit this ugly death? Aisa had believed in justice, and history, and his life had been thrown away like a crumpled ball of paper! Faisal's entire being raged against it. Who could have foreseen such a thing? He, Faisal, might die, but not Aisa, who was so convinced of the rightness of their cause, whose clarity of mind had supported Faisal at every turn. Thinking of that ghastly face (not Aisa's face at all, Faisal protested, that grisly death mask!), he felt himself suffocating with grief and rage. And the pilot who had killed him? What of him? Would Faisal ever have any more than a hollow, symbolic revenge, killing some other, meaningless Jew to atone for the wanton, precise murder committed a hundred feet above the Jordan? What were his chances of meeting that man, except as Aisa had met him, through the spider-web sights of an aircraft machine gun? Faisal's rage was redoubled with impotence. Even this easy night march into Israel struck him now as an insult, as the open contempt of the Jew for the Fatah, as if their very carelessness said, Come, we invite you! March to your deaths! We are waiting for you, we, the Sons of Abraham, the Chosen, with our tanks, and our jets, our rockets, our pride and fierceness. And Aisa falling hopelessly into the river, splashing face down through the water with his hands clutching his torn throat and the helicopter banking out of its dive, Aisa floating then, motionless, turning with the slow brown current, his arms outstretched and blood gushing into the muddy water, and the pilot leaning back easily on the controls, turning coolly to strafe the survivors. If he could meet that Jew, Faisal thought, face to face! His mind burning, he felt something of Hamad's hatred of helicopters, though with none of Hamad's religious awe, none of his holy dread. What Faisal felt was, instead, a direct and absolute desire to murder.

Ali took the squad up over another low ridge, crossing higher this time than they had before and then down a footpath, where they turned northward and saw a squat, flat silhouette looming ahead of them. This was Mount Allafet. Again in the south lay a wider blackness, a long, spreading valley where clusters of lights twinkled in the heat. Bearing steadily away from them, they crossed the southern flank of the hill. Faisal locked his thumbs against his shoulder straps to anchor his forward-straining arms. To the left he saw a line of tall, dark shapes sticking up against the sky. Were they telephone poles? No, too close together—poplar trees, forming a windbreak. There would be a road on the other side. The Captain avoided the line of trees. They moved to the right and hastened away, navigating through a new labyrinth of ravines. They emerged into a grove of pine trees, their boots raising puffs of dust and dry needles. Faisal felt the ground sloping down and then again there was soft, level earth underfoot. Everything about them now lay in total blackness. Not a single light marked the horizon. They crossed the monotony of another open field, where again he felt the momentary, foot-by-foot dread that he had felt in the river, the certainty that if Ali did not slow down they would all plunge into some devilishly prepared trap, tumble into a pit, walk off a cliff, find themselves colliding against a stone wall. It seemed that they had come miles from the river, yet Ali never stopped, never used a light, never looked at a map. Faisal struggled as if he were drowning; his breath came in short gasps; his ribs ached as if they had been hammered on both sides; his boots were puddled with sweat. Behind him he heard Hamad still laboring to keep up. Ahead, the taller figure of Salah bobbed up and down with a half-crippled, jerky walk of a manikin. Each time they went over a rise Faisal saw Salah's silhouette caught momentarily against the faintly starry sky before he dropped down again out of sight. Faisal followed, his heart constricting when he exposed himself in the same way until he plunged into the surrounding blackness, his lungs and face seared as if he were marching in a furnace.

They had come an hour in the direction of Beit Shal when Ali called the first halt. The squad rested at the edge of an open field, under the embankment of a dirt road. Faisal noted with satisfaction that even the Captain was winded.

"The Valley of the Jezzine is ahead," Ali said. "We must get through the farms before moonrise. We will move faster from here on."

Faisal sank down on one knee, loosening his shoulder straps, his chest heaving with exertion. He slid his Sten gun off his arm, wondering how they could possibly move even faster. Salah threw himself on the ground beside him, grunting with pain.

"What's the matter?" Faisal asked.

"Nothing," Salah gasped, spreading his arms and legs out as if he were crucified. "I twisted my foot." He groaned with self-derision. "It doesn't matter . . . those filthy ravines."

Hamad crouched near them, like a half-wild animal seeking the comfort of men. He was wheezing (the greater weight of his explosives, the C-4 mine, thought Faisal, ashamed of his own fatigue, and remembering Hamad's shorter legs), but he found enough breath to whisper:

"I have dropped something."

Before Faisal could answer, Salah sat bolt upright. His voice was an outraged whisper. "What is it, you mule?"

"I don't know. I felt it come off the pack. It hung down for a while; then it dropped."

"But where?"

"Far back," Hamad replied evasively.

Salah jerked him around and fumbled angrily over his pack, counting the bundles of explosives. "Jackass, why didn't you say something?"

"I was in the river. There was no time."

Ali looked on with professional stoicism. "Never mind," he said, removing the lost equipment from his calculations, thought Faisal, as easily as he would have eliminated Hamad if he had fallen behind. "We couldn't have stopped for it. Can you tell what is missing?"

"Not without a light," Salah answered bitterly. His

voice was sour, as if he wanted to tongue-lash Hamad the way he would have a student who had carelessly smashed an expensive test tube. It would not have mattered if Hamad had lost his Sten gun, his ammunition belt, or even himself; but Hamad had lost a piece of Salah's explosive apparatus, he had upset its perfect symmetry, and for that Salah would never forgive him. "It was the C-4 detonator," he said at last. "It was here with the timers for the bridge plastic, now it's gone." He cursed quietly and steadily. "You peasant's left foot, your straps were tight! I checked them myself!"

"They were too tight," Hamad admitted. "I loosened them in the river."

Salah exploded. "Why, in the name of God?"

"I thought I would drown."

"Do you hear that? The mule thought he would drown!" Salah groaned. "Then why didn't you slip the whole pack and drown? At least we would have had the detonator!"

"That's enough," Ali ordered curtly, getting up from his short rest, leaning on his machine gun. "I tell you it makes no difference. Keep your voice down. He has not lost any plastic, has he?"

"No," Salah admitted grudgingly. "But when the towers at Beit Shal blow up, the Jew is going to come at us down an open road that ought to have been blown to Hell. Do you think he can fire that mine by spitting on it?"

"Forget the mine," Ali said. "We have no choice now."

Salah persisted. "We could use plastic on the culvert!"

"We don't have enough. The towers come first."

"Then scratch one tower," Salah argued, "and do the road."

"Forget it," Ali said. "That's an order. The drainage tunnel was the least important part of our plan." Salah protested angrily, reluctant to give up the scenario of his idealized explosions, the choreography of stunning surprises, but the Captain ignored him, and at last Salah lapsed into brooding silence. As if to console him, Ali added, "The road was too risky anyway. We want to stay away from that garrison."

Salah remained bitter. "No, we want that garrison to stay away from *us*. Now, thanks to Hamad, there's nothing to stop them coming straight down that road out of Beit Shal."

Faisal had listened indifferently to this argument over lost equipment. It was nothing to him whether they mined a culvert drainpipe or an electrical tower. He rested on one knee to ease the strain of his shoulder straps, his head down, his eyes nearly shut with exhaustion. Listening thus, he was the first to hear the voices overhead.

He grabbed Ali's arm. *"Captain,"* he whispered.

"What is it?"

"Up there—someone's on the road!"

The squad lay in frozen silence for a moment, flattened against the embankment. Then Ali crawled noiselessly up to the roadbed. A moment later he dropped down. "A truck," he said, "a hundred yards to the left."

"Army?"

"I couldn't tell."

Footsteps came toward them, passed overhead, stopped, as if the Jew were looking up and down the road, and then came slowly back.

A muffled voice said, ". . . bad piece of luck, just the same."

From the truck there came a scratching metallic sound, as if a hubcap were being pried off with a tire iron. Something clattered onto the road; a ratchet went to work. Faisal pressed his face against the hard earth of the embankment, his heart pounding, his Sten gun held tightly across his chest, wondering if the Captain would order them to fight. If it was an army truck setting up a roadblock, they would be trapped. He nudged Salah, indicating with a sweep of his hand that they could move left to outflank the truck. Salah shook his head; they were better off where they were. A second voice came from the road.

". . . main thing is not to let them catch you like this. That's the main thing. After all, they mean business, too. Look here, can't you do anything properly?"

"This filthy wrench," said the other voice.

"Well," the first replied, quite calmly, "try the smaller one."

"Filthy night for this . . . Fucking black, I can't see. Can't you help me? Fucking patrols will be along—"

A hammer went to work tapping a metallic object. Something heavy was dragged off the truck bed. Muffled grunts of exertion; then, again, the tapping. A third voice, huskier, laughed. "Never find it in there."

Faisal groaned inwardly, hardly able to restrain himself. A horrible sense of the fallibility of even the most scrupulous planning overcame his caution. They were barely three miles inside Israel, and already trapped. Everything was at an end. He wanted to leap to his feet, shouting, to open fire at once, to strafe the road recklessly and kill as many of the enemy as they could. Why should they wait to be discovered, cowering like dogs? They could sweep these few off the road as if they were using a high-pressure hose. After that . . . Well, Faisal told himself, he had never expected to reach Beit Shal alive anyway.

Footsteps ran toward the truck. A door slammed. "Chaim, you crazy? . . . get caught out here!"

The reply was a laugh. "That won't rattle—"

Another door slammed, and the heavy engine turned over. Faisal waited in suspense for the lights to flare up; if there was a curvature to the roadbed they would be caught in full view on the embankment; he heard a dull snap as the bolt of the Captain's machine gun came off safety. But the truck rumbled by overhead without turning on its headlights. When it was gone Ali stood up and looked around. Only the fading sound of the engine told the direction the road took.

"Well, you are some lucky Jews," Ali muttered, "that's all I've got to say. You are some damn lucky Jews."

Faisal, his Sten gun still gripped tensely in both hands, came up beside him. "What were they?" he asked.

"Smugglers, I suppose," replied Ali, "running hashish."

"Then they weren't soldiers?"

"Jews all the same. Wouldn't that have been pretty?" the Captain added with cryptic dryness, leaving Faisal to wonder what he meant by pretty, that the Fatah squad might have been caught in the sweep of the truck's headlights in plain view at the side of the road, arguing like truant schoolboys over lost detonators, or to have machine-gunned the unsuspecting Jews out of sheer vexation with Hamad's stupidity and Salah's petulance. Faisal was not sure whether they or the Jews on the road had been the luckier.

Without another word Ali moved away into the darkness. The others scrambled across the road and followed him. Faisal heard Salah swearing, and took his arm. "You all right?" he asked. "Can you walk?"

"I can walk! Leave me alone!" Salah groaned audibly. "That idiot Syrian—what kind of soldier is he? Why does he think we're breaking our backs to get this stuff to Beit Shal?" Then, venting his rage on the only thing conveniently to hand, the smugglers who had almost discovered them on the road: "I'd like to have shot that damn truck up! Shot it straight to Hell!" Salah slowed down, still limping with his great, awkward stride, and fell in behind Hamad. "Drop anything you like now, mule. I'm going to be behind you all the way."

"Must I carry the mine?" Hamad asked. "It won't do us any good now."

"Drop that mine and I'll cut your throat!" Salah snarled. "You carried it this far, you can carry it all the way back to El Husn. You think we've got stuff like that to throw away?"

Hamad said nothing. Faisal, leaving the two of them to their private war, hastened on to close up behind the Captain. Incredibly, the night seemed to have become hotter; a dry, parchmentlike wind stirred over the fields, blowing up funnels of dust. The heat rose under their faces in nauseating waves. Faisal heard Hamad's canteen open . . . the clanking of the unscrewed cap, the gurgling sounds of drinking on the move, water spilling, Hamad choking. Now that the immediate danger of the road was past, his own fatigue welled over him with a dreamlike, stupefying desperation. He felt as if the shock of their near discovery had squandered his last ounce of energy. Again, the principal enemy was the march (I will not let Ali outmarch me, I will not let him outmarch

me!). It was exactly, Faisal thought, like walking over
the lid of an oven, although it was no longer a walk.
Making up for the time lost at the road, the Captain had
increased the pace until they were trotting, their boots
thudding in the soft earth of a plowed field, their mouths
open, teeth bared, gasping for breath, equipment thump-
ing with dull, padded abrasions of canvas on rubber,
making, all of them, the muted shuffling sounds of a
string of convicts being transported through Hell. When
they were safely across the fields, Ali slowed, and, as if
with extrasensory vision, led them safely into the mouth
of a dry riverbed. Here they were hidden on both sides
by the eroded bank. The sandy bottom led them westward. Fifteen minutes later, climbing for a long distance,
they left the gulley and reached the top of a ridge of
stony hills, the Captain winding back and forth on the
down slope. Faisal stumbled after him, his mind flaring
with the blind, dry rage of exhaustion. Like Salah, he
found himself thinking in a dreamlike trance of the Jews
they had encountered on the road, of red tracers snap-
ping off from Sten guns, gliding in their long graceful arc
to shatter and ignite the metallic parts of the truck. His
mind dwelt on it, fascinated, while his body lurched after
the tireless figure of the Captain, who marched with the
iron regularity of a piston. More than once he heard
Salah stumble and get up cursing, to drive Hamad on
with redoubled fury. Again they entered open fields,
where they broke into a full run until at last they reached
the shelter of an olive grove.

Sensing that Ali meant to stop, Faisal splashed through
a shallow water ditch and threw himself at full length
onto the bank, his face pressed against the wet grass.

As if from afar, he heard Ali say:

"Over there are the lights of Kibbutz Ben-Gurion."
He added, without the least sign of irony, "It will be on
your left coming out. It will be your guide. Remember
it."

Faisal grunted and rolled over heavily. When he sat up
he saw clusters of lights in the distance. Beyond the dark
grove the westward horizon was lined with rows of
poplar trees; they followed the undulations of the un-
even ground like fence palings. Irrigation canals lay close
by, and fields of ripe cabbages and melons—Faisal could
smell the fetid dark water, the green odors of farming.
They were in the Jezzine now, among the settlements.
The border zone of stones and dry wadis, that no man's
land of patrols and ambushes, was behind them. This was
truly Israel, and Faisal found himself staring at it with as
much curiosity as antagonism. It was like stepping forth
onto the dark side of the moon.

When they had taken three minutes rest the Captain
went straight ahead, the squad strung out behind in a
ragged line, keeping a little to the south to maintain an
even distance between the lighted farms. They passed a
pumping station; they could hear the regular pulse of the
diesels. It was less than a quarter mile away—Faisal could
see the water in the main irrigation canal reflecting the
light atop the pump house. Surely there would be guards
there. The Jew might be careless along the Jordan,
knowing that he could never guard it effectively against
the commandos' determination to cross, but he would be
on the alert in this rich valley. Faisal imagined the pleasure of blowing up the canal and flooding the ripe fields,
saw, in his mind's eye, the white flash, the orange blast of
flame a microsecond later, the concussion of broken fragments, like smashed crockery rising in a cloud of dust

and smoke, the surrounding blackness framed in that lurid light, followed by the arrival of the sonic blast, making the front of one's clothing jump, the heart skip a beat out of fear and delight. He wished ardently that this was what they had come for, not because of his fatigue, nor out of fear of what awaited them at Beit Shal, but because this fat, sleeping vision of Israel infuriated him. He wanted to burst this calm with the flash and thud of *plastiques*, to shatter that offensive, domestic slumber. The sight of the fully lit canal affected him strangely. Most of all, it insulted him. It outraged him to be crossing these rich farms like a thief while their new owners slept in soft beds, next to soft women, in those dark, ample farm buildings which they had stolen from Arabs. More strongly than ever before, Faisal suffered the hatred of the dispossessed. These fields had once belonged to his people. His own family's land, near Tiberias, the stone house and barely remembered olive terraces, was not far to the north. Yet if it infuriated him to steal through the farms, an intruder on his own land, it doubled his rage, made it truly unbearable, to cross them with such impunity. Was it thus that the arrogant Jew showed his contempt? Was he so secure in this stolen valley that he felt no need to stand guard? Well, then, thought Faisal, Kassim was right! Strike at Beit Shal! Strike through the soft white underbelly of sleeping Jezzine! Wake these complacent Jews with the roar of mines! For one moment, perhaps, he understood Salah's almost mystical reverence for the burden of explosives they carried, for here was the final, persuasive voice of revenge. Not even the Jew could ignore it. The Jew relied on war? Very well, they would give him war! Faisal conceived an intense, almost personal hatred for the electrical towers at Beit Shal. He

had thought that he was marching into Israel for an abstract principle; now, watching the lighted pumping station slip by unmolested, he understood, with a strange
unexpected relief, that like all the others he fought
merely out of anger, and grief, and shame, the torments
of exile for which there were no words.

When they came to a run of hedgerows Ali led them
into the narrowest part of the valley, where it formed a
funnel with the dark shoulders of steep hills on both
sides, blocking out the stars of the lower sky, and enclos-
ing them like walls. Faisal remembered having looked at
this place on the topographical map in the operations tent
with a sense of unreality. "The bottleneck," he had
called it. Now, feeling no more real than he had then, he
unlimbered his Sten gun, eased it down into the crook of
his arm, and slid the bolt off safety.

When they were nearly through the valley a dog
barked nearby. Ali dropped down on one knee, and
waited. The dog barked again, this time closer. Faisal
crept forward until his outstretched hand touched a wall.
The wall was old, of unmortared stone. An Arab wall.

Now the dog was running in circles, barking frantically. It would awaken the whole valley; Faisal wondered if the Captain would kill it; tensely he waited for
him to act. Suddenly an electric light was switched on,
disclosing a house startlingly close by. A door opened
less than fifty yards from them. A slender figure stood
silhouetted in the rectangle of light thrown out into the
darkness. Behind, on a wooden table where a chair had
been pushed back, stood a bottle of wine and a white
plate. A hushed voice called out to the dog.

"Farhousha! *Farhousha!*"

Instinctively, Faisal raised his gun to the firing position, sighting against the doorway with his elbows braced on the stone wall. Mentally, as if he were still on the target range, he registered the neutral fact that at that distance the Sten gun, never as accurate as, though much quicker than, a rifle, would spray the entire doorway with bullets. One would have to depress the sights to keep from overshooting. To hit a lighted target at night, he told himself, pretend you are shooting downhill. Carefully, in order to hit the chest, Faisal aimed for the knees.

The dog ran gratefully inside the house, its tail between its legs, whining. For a moment longer the figure stood in the light, hesitating, peering out into the blackness. Then the Jew reached slowly for the switch and turned off the light, plunging the house once again into such total darkness that Faisal doubted for a moment that he had seen it at all. The door closed. Shaken, Faisal lowered his gun. He had wanted to fire; he had wanted desperately to fire; he had wanted to fire so badly that now, as in the aftermath of rage or passion, his limbs felt weak and his mouth was as dry as ash. The Jew had been unarmed, yet all the frustration of the night, Aisa's tortured face, the regular pulse of the engines at the pumping station, had gathered to release itself in that simple act of squeezing a trigger. Another second, Faisal thought, and he would surely have stitched that lighted doorway with bullets.

Faisal stood up, awaiting the Captain's order to move on, but before he could turn away a flashlight appeared where the house had stood. It approached the wall, swung across the hedges with an interrogative glance, then moved over the open ground in slow circles, advancing. The Jew had remained outside. At last the slender beam of light lifted upward. Faisal, caught standing behind the wall, froze with the light shining directly in his face.

A hushed voice called out, "Who's there? Rabin, is that you?"

Faisal could not move, nor, apparently, could the other—the light tethered both of them unwaveringly. Faisal stared into its blinding center with mute fascination, his hands gripping his Sten gun lifelessly, as incapable of firing it now as if he had never touched a gun in his life. He felt his arms bound by the knowledge that something awful was about to happen, yet would happen without his having to act (indeed, he would not be allowed to act), and it was this quality of nightmare that held him paralyzed.

Again the Jew called, this time more urgently, "Who is it? What do you want?"

The fragile beam of light held Faisal's face for no more than ten seconds, though to him it seemed that whole minutes had passed in agony before the light suddenly lurched forward and dropped to the ground with a violent, outward toss. There was a struggle, a dull thud, followed by a muffled gasp. Something held the Jew's body upright for a moment, then released it. When it fell the face lay in the beam of light. A pair of gold-rimmed eyeglasses dangled from one ear. The eyes were open in astonishment. The face was young, no older than Faisal himself, who stared at it fixedly for the brief seconds before the Captain's boot came down on the flashlight with a heavy crunch. Indelibly printed on Faisal's memory, the scene vanished into darkness.

Ali turned to him angrily. "Why did you let him see you? Why did you stand there?"

"But I was going to shoot," Faisal said weakly.

"Shoot?" the Captain hissed. "Next time use your knife, you idiot. Your knife!"

"I forgot," Faisal whispered absurdly, shaking his head.

Ali's voice was cold. "So I observed. Next time don't leave your dirty work for me to do!"

"But, my God! . . ." Faisal gasped, trembling. He felt himself choking. What had this Jew to do with him? "We didn't—!"

"There was no choice."

Faisal protested. "We could have tied him. We could . . ."

"*Shut up.*"

The Jewish youth was still moving beneath them. There was a throaty, gurgling noise. Horrified, Faisal listened to the sounds of a human being inhaling, and choking on liquidity.

"Finish him," Ali said.

"I can't."

"Finish him!"

"No . . . not with a knife." Faisal offered weakly: "I could shoot him. But not the knife!"

"*Damn* you," said Ali, and quickly stopped the struggle. He turned the body (so Faisal conjectured, the ruffled sounds of clothing and boots turning, the dull thud of weight) and drove his knife into the Jew's chest. The sound of it was solid, emphatic, and dull, like a blade penetrating wet sand. No one said a word. There was no final cry. Everything had been accomplished in less than two minutes. Within the darkened house only the dog was left howling.

The Captain and Hamad dragged the body into the hedges, where they rolled it into a ditch and covered it with branches. They waited for several minutes longer;

then, satisfied that no one else had seen them, Ali gave Faisal a rough shove forward. "Come on. Get moving."

Faisal fell in behind the Captain, every nerve in his body cruelly tensed until they were safely across the last open ground. Soon they had put the farms behind them, but the memory of the face lying in the beam of light, the eyes staring with disbelief, would not leave him. Slowly, it dawned on him what had held the Jew in such stupefied, lethal wonder. Faisal saw what the other had seen—his own face blackened with grease, beyond human recognition, or the claim of any human sympathy; the guerrilla's camouflage suit; the Sten gun leveled to fire; the deadly thought *Al Fatah* slowly taking shape, almost too frightening for belief. Certainly too frightening to be believed quickly enough. The face the Jewish youth had seen had been (so Faisal felt, regarding himself with a shiver) the face of Death. He had stared at Faisal with shuddering disbelief, and then behind him had come the swift shadow of the Captain, the powerful arm locked at his throat, cutting off his last cry, the knife driven with murderous force between his ribs.

With murderous force, Faisal thought—for that was the only category under which he could comprehend what had happened. It had been a murder.

He felt chilled and humiliated. The Jew had not been armed, of that he was sure; yet what if he had carried a rifle? What if he had been a militiaman? If he had been in uniform, Faisal wondered, could he have killed him? He groaned inwardly, his thoughts twisting to escape the dilemma of his own inaction. He had raised the Sten gun out of sheer instinct. He had not even thought of his knife. Yet it was a shock, mortal and irreconcilable, to have seen the open eyes staring into the light, for that

dying face reminded him of Aisa. Faisal could not say if
it was Ali's act, or his own fear, that humiliated him the
most. He tried to put the whole incident out of his mind
as something shameful, merely an accident—yet he could
not escape the throaty, gushing sound of the drowning
Jew.

Involuntarily, his pulse beating angrily in his temples,
he wondered about the others. Hamad, he thought,
might as well be mad. He would not have killed him.
Only his own death interested him. He had come in
search of his peculiar God. "Are you the one?" he might
have asked, wondering if this dark emissary with the
flashlight was the angel sent to bring him before his
Maker. And Salah, too, even the educated Salah served a
half-mad ideal; like Hamad, he loved more than he hated,
though his love was reserved for the lyrical violence of
his *plastiques,* and to this the Jew was irrelevant. Ali
could kill, of course, of that Faisal had never doubted,
though he had silenced the youth out of sheer military
efficiency, without anger or remorse. A job to be done.
Unpleasant but, under the circumstances, necessary. And
then Faisal thought once more of Aisa. Why had Aisa
died in the Jordan? Why had the Jew come to stand so
stupidly before him with a flashlight? What had his murder accomplished but to double the horror of Aisa's
death? Faisal had wanted no revenge from the youth
with the gold-rimmed eyeglasses, and the dog named
Farhousha. In his heart he blamed the Jews bitterly for
both tragedies, the death of his friend, this unnecessary
death at Jezzine. Didn't they know enough to keep in-
doors at night?

Faisal stayed penitently close to the Captain, his head
down, unable to explain himself. Why *had* he stood

there? Why hadn't he killed the Jew? After all, he was a Fatah; this was what he had come for. He let his thoughts flare angrily, and the strong, anguished hate came back. He felt confused, bitter, the prey to many sudden doubts. Most of all he cursed the Jews, for they tormented him with questions that he did not want to answer.

The Bridge

"BEIT SHAL lies on the other side of that hill," said Ali, crouching at the edge of a creek that ran through the orchard and went down onto the plain. "The road divides there. One fork goes south, toward Allenby; the other turns around the hill and passes directly through Beit Shal. This creekbed runs down under the bridge. If any of you are coming back alone, the creek is the fastest way out. Remember it."

"And the bridge?" asked Salah, edging forward to where the Captain knelt, leaning with both hands on the barrel of his machine gun.

"You can see it down in that hollow, there, where the plain goes into shadow. It's a mile from here." Ali laid his machine gun down on the ground and rested against a tree, totally worn out. He ripped his collar open, exposing a triangle of white undershirt with his grease-blackened hand.

The squad of Al Fatah had made the bridge at moonrise, almost to the minute. Coming through the last mile of the valley Ali had clung to the low ground, running them through water ditches, culverts, under road embankments, twisting with the shadows of orchards to avoid the open ground where they might be seen. An orange grove stood in dark shadow at the end of the valley, and they rested in it. Now the open space beyond the orange trees lay in a pale, dusty light. Faisal looked warily over his shoulder; a full moon, swollen and reddened by the atmosphere, stood clear of the horizon. It cast an orange haze over the distant hills, rank upon rank of serrated crests, like waves of the sea. That way lay Jordan, and safety. Ahead, across the flat, shadowed plain, stood a round-topped hill with a flashing radio beacon. In the orchard the ground was dappled with spots of moonlight.

"Get your charges ready," Ali said. "I want no time wasted down there. You won't have any cover except the shadow of the bridge itself. We have exactly one hour to reach Beit Shal and get to work; there's a moon now, and we're going to be slower. I'll give you fifteen minutes under the bridge. If you aren't finished, we go on." Ali checked his watch. "It's 2300. We begin work on the towers at midnight, and will be out of Beit Shal and back into the Jezzine by 0200. Set your charges to fire the bridge at 0215."

Salah was busy shifting equipment from Hamad's pack to his own. He tied the plastics loosely together, and bundled them in two separate oilskin sacks. "Don't worry, they will blow on time," he said, unwrapping the detonators. He removed one, and carefully repacked the rest. "When do the charges at Beit Shal go off?"

"At 0200," said Ali.

Salah glanced at him doubtfully. "You don't think the Jews can get to the bridge before 0215?"

"I expect them to arrive there thirty minutes after the blast. They'll have to organize their patrols." The Captain added dryly, "They are only human."

Salah shrugged. "In that case, the bridge goes at 0215 on the dot, guaranteed. Who knows?" He grinned wolfishly. "Maybe we'll catch Dayan on his way home from a whore."

Faisal, who had been kneeling beside the silent Hamad, now looked up. His thoughts were still occupied with the dead Jew. He was not so much thinking about what had happened—indeed, the youth dead, what was there to think about?—as brooding darkly. But now the urgency of the task immediately ahead drove him to focus his attention on what the Captain and Salah were saying.

He moved closer, with a shuffling of boots on the dry leaves of the orchard floor. "But why not detonate the bridge at the same time as the towers?"

"I want the Jew to have fifteen minutes after the towers blow up," Ali explained, "before he'll know what direction we've taken. Some of his patrols will start out along other routes and have to turn back. Of course, he'll assume that we have made for the river, but he can't *know* until the bridge explodes. It gives us just that much more time. He might also think there's more than one raiding party, and hold back some of his pursuit to cover other targets. Beit Shal is a fat plum. There is a hospital and orphanage. We want the Jew to worry."

"So we have two hours," said Faisal, "to get out of the Jezzine before the Beit Shal mines go off." He felt a cold, solid dread creep into his bones at the thought of returning through Jezzine, of actually trespassing again on that farm where the body lay covered in the hedgerow. Suddenly he remembered the dog locked in the house, and wondered if it would still be howling, the ghost of the murdered Jew drifting past the windows.

Ali corrected him. "One hour. We won't get off the hill until 0100."

With an urgency that had escaped him in the operations tent that afternoon, Faisal now found himself, in the obscure shadows of the orchard, calculating the distances and timing of the raid. They were alarmingly out of agreement.

"But why not set all the mines, and towers and the bridge, to explode tomorrow morning," he suggested, "when we're across the river?"

"There are going to be sentries at those towers," Ali said. "They might spot the mines."

"But, still . . ."

"No, I won't risk delaying the firing more than two hours. We count on Salah to hide the plastic—yes, I know, Salah, you can do it!—but still there is a risk." He added with a shrug, as if admitting the obvious: "It is a compromise between getting across the river alive, and being sure of the towers."

Still Faisal wanted to protest—why bother with the bridge at all if they were going to be an hour on the far side of it? Why tell the Jews the direction they had taken? Nothing made sense to him any longer; he should never have committed himself to the raid; there was a logical flaw. He had the giddy feeling that in another moment he would grasp it, and explain everything to the Captain. But the logical flaw, he knew, was his own desire to live. He did not want to die, not after what had happened in Jezzine.

"I only meant," he replied soberly, "that if we leave the bridge standing, they might think we've gone into hiding in an Arab settlement. They would have to scatter their pursuit."

"You're mistaken," Ali replied with a patience that surprised Faisal. "The Jew will send a strong patrol down that road, and into the Jezzine, no matter what we do at the bridge. And he'll alert every garrison between Beit Shal and the Jordan to be on the lookout for us. A half hour after the mines go off, he'll have helicopters dropping flares all over the West Bank. If he doesn't find us by morning he'll have plenty of time to take the Arab settlements apart." Ali shifted his position, tightening his field pack with an air of cutting off further discussion. "We are going to draw hot pursuit no matter what we do—and I want that bridge cut to slow down whatever part of it comes out of Beit Shal. That will be the hornet's nest. After all, if we wanted to be absolutely sure of getting out alive," Ali said, standing up slowly, "we wouldn't blow the towers. So it is a compromise. Only remember," he added, looking down at Faisal, "that the towers come first; our getting across the river is secondary. It is that kind of compromise."

"I heard the Major," said Faisal manfully. "We're expendable. I understand that."

There was almost a trace of a smile in Ali's voice. "We're not the only ones," he said.

Faisal turned to look blankly down into the dark flat before them, a small, cramped plain wedged narrowly between steep, rugged hills where Ali said the bridge, and the first step of the raid itself, awaited them. Faisal knew that once they left the shelter of the orchard everything would begin. All that had seemed merely problematical would now become irreversible. For a moment he wondered if Hamad could see the track of fate down which they were about to walk, the accidents which would not be accidents at all, the mistakes which had already been determined by them, or for them— whether in the stars, or in the cumulative effect of their own decisions, made little difference as far as Faisal could see. The end result, life or death, was always the same, regardless of the explanation—God, Fate, or dumb chance—that you put upon it. Probably some of them were going to die. The idea, taken suddenly out of the abstract and made real, struck him as a logical absurdity, as if the word itself, "death," had no meaning. It was the absolute Unknown, as pointless as infinity, the last concept of lost, finite minds. Only when he thought of Aisa did he feel that he could comprehend at least one part of death. It was a terrible emptiness, the welling, deep ache in those who survived, the suffering of a small animal unable to understand the cause of its own pain. The memory of Aisa's face now filled him with revulsion. He found, having reached the bridge, that he was possessed oddly of nothing more heroic than a strong desire to be finished. Calculating their chances, he felt as if he were weighing the lives of strangers. None of it was any longer real to him. The Jewish youth in Jezzine had stolen his rage, and with it his belief, for he discovered now that he could not think of Aisa without thinking also of that face staring into the flashlight. He felt inwardly crippled. Every aspect of the raid began to dissatisfy him —the long march into Israel; the Captain's military, almost comic-opera, love of split-second timing (Could any of them come out from Beit Shal that quickly? What was to prevent them from being trapped, or delayed, and reaching the bridge at 0215 themselves, to be absurdly blown to pieces in their own mines?); the waiting electrical towers; the Captain, Salah, Hamad, even himself (himself, he wondered, most of all?) left him feeling stale, suspicious, cold. Why was he in Israel? How had this happened to him? His back was awash with sweat. His shirt clung to him with a clammy, revolting touch. Grimly, Faisal told himself that he would do his job; he would do it thoroughly, in a businesslike manner; and then he would get out, perhaps in the light of another day, once more safely in his tent at El Husn, to comprehend the source of this detached mood which had suddenly made him see the Fatah patrol, and above all himself, from the uncomfortable distance of a skeptical judge. The darkness seemed to him the perfect metaphor for the confusion and anger into which his soul had been led. The one death that no man could envision, Faisal reflected honestly, was his own.

Salah clapped him on the shoulder. "Don't worry about the Jews, they don't need us to tell them which direction we'll take. Where do we little Fatahs always run when we've blown up one of their nice toys? He laughed quietly. "Straight for the river. Like lemmings."

Salah found Faisal in no mood for this military, Devil-may-care humor. It struck him as British, mawkish, horribly false, considering what they had just done, and were about to do. Yet Salah's spirits had genuinely risen. With work before them, and the misery of marching at the Captain's killing pace at least temporarily at an end, Salah seemed hardly to remember his swollen ankle, or the body at Jezzine. After all, he'd had nothing to do with that; it wasn't his job even to have an opinion about

it. Let the Captain handle that. His sole job was the engi-
neering of exquisite explosions, nothing more. Waiting
beside Faisal, his agile body emanating the strength of
tall, angular men whose sinews and muscles are tensed
for some desperate leap, Salah readied his plastics, eager
to construct the first of his apparently simple, deceptively
complex explosions. "If it hadn't been for the mule we
would have given the Jew a bloody nose every time he
turned around. A pity," he added philosophically, "but
there you are."

"It doesn't matter."

Salah grinned at him. "You worried, little brother?"

"Of course I'm worried," Faisal said. "I want to have it
finished."

"And indeed we shall." Salah smiled cryptically. "Indeed we shall."

Faisal turned away from Salah's grin, which was a reflex, fierce, cannibal-looking, yet wholly involuntary,
the physical effect of nervous strain. Faisal had crossed
the Jordan with a knife between his teeth, it was true,
bent on revenge. But now with his rage cooled it un-
nerved him to think that his friend could enjoy any part
of the raid, and it was exactly the low parody of the mad
bomber in Salah's smile, the glint of iron in the eye, that
made him look away.

"Are you packed up?" Ali asked.

"Ready," said Salah.

"Then let's get started."

Ali led them out of the shadow of the orchard and
across the first stretch of open ground. A lunar landscape
of small stones, boulders, eroded ledges of sand where
the rains had cut the plain slipped behind them, bathed in
moonlight. The full illumination was shocking after their

long effort to hug the shadows of ravines and orchards,
Even when they went down into the creekbed, moving
doubled over, keeping their heads under the cover of the
dry brush that clung to the upper ledge, they found no
real shelter. Faisal watched the banks of fragile reeds, the
water glistening in the moonlit eddies as it flowed over
rocks and pebbly moraines; ahead of him the Captain's
broad back was clearly visible; with a shudder, he wondered who was watching his own back. Salah? Or a Jewish militiaman, looming suddenly over them with a sub-
machine gun? Faisal felt the same panic that had nearly
overcome him in the river, the momentary, foot-by-foot
dread that they were walking into a trap. In the river he
had wanted to take a breath and shout; now he opened
his eyes wider, like a boxer trying to foresee the split-
second hesitation of his opponent, to slip inside his timing
and deliver the first lethal blow. Their only defense now
would be the quickness of their vision, the advantage of
surprise. He kept pace silently behind Ali, avoiding the
eddies of the creek where his boots might splash, starting
at every sound, his Sten gun at the ready. If he did not
see his enemy first, he thought, he would be dead.

Ali halted a thousand yards short of the bridge. They
could see it more clearly now, rising a little higher than
the embankments of the creek it traversed. It was a
simple stone arch, with low abutments, its total span
hardly more than fifty feet, yet it was obvious that its
demolition would stop any wheeled vehicles from crossing the ravine. Grudgingly, Faisal admitted the sound-
ness of Ali's planning; if they got this far, only foot soldiers could continue the chase.

The Captain motioned for Salah to come up with him.
"You too, Faisal. Cover him under the bridge. Hamad

and I will wait here. If you run into trouble, we will try to help you, otherwise we will go on to Beit Shal alone or head back for the river. If there are sentries, take them silently. I'll give you fifteen minutes."

"You're coming down the ravine?"

Ali nodded. "Under the bridge, but not until you have been there fifteen minutes. And then we go straight on." He indicated the upper embankment with the stock of his machine gun. "There's nothing up there but open country until we reach Beit Shal. We'll follow the ravine all the way in."

Salah lifted his oilskin sacks to his shoulder, bent double, and was off down the sandy bank of the creek without a word, his body swinging and his hands touching the ground ahead of him, moving with an efficient simian, perfectly soundless shuffle, the sacks of explosives slung from one shoulder swaying under him, and his Sten gun hanging by its leather strap from the other. He looked to Faisal, who came a few paces behind, like a maternal predator, with her young clinging to her underside, rocking in peaceful slumber while she stalked her nocturnal prey. Then Faisal looked up, irritated that he had allowed himself this image; there was nothing metaphoric about the bridge, which emerged out of the semidarkness with greater detail as they approached. Soon the individual stones were visible; there was patchwork on one side where the new mortar stood out white in the moonlight; the older blocks, under the capstone of the arch and along the guardrail, were a dull gray. In daylight, Faisal thought, they would be red.

They had approached to within a hundred yards of the bridge, putting a shoulder of the embankment between themselves and the Captain, when Salah suddenly dropped into the shadows of the ledge. There were head-lights moving on the road. Faisal dropped down quickly behind him, his heart pounding. When they could hear the engine—it was small, perhaps a civilian motorcar, or an army Jeep—Faisal heard the bolt of Salah's gun snick back. He gripped Salah's arm from behind and forced it down. "Are you crazy?" he whispered. "Let it go by. It's nothing, just a motorcar." The headlights swung momentarily in their direction, too feeble to penetrate more than a few dozen yards over their heads, flared, and then turned away after slowing almost to a stop on the approach of the bridge. The vehicle went out of sight above them with a blink of orange taillights.

Relieved, Faisal let go of Salah's arm. "For the love of God, were you really going to fire on them? It was just a Jeep."

"They can do what they like," Salah muttered, "it's their country. Only not here, damn it! Not here! Not now!" He added darkly, "Not when I've got this bridge to mine."

"You won't mine it if you're *dead*."

The danger past, Salah's humor returned. "Were you scared, baby?" he asked, taking a hidden, sidelong glance at Faisal.

"And you weren't?"

Salah laughed. "Not for a minute. Just a farmer going home. Nothing to worry about."

"Just keep that grease gun of yours silent."

Salah's reply was sardonic: "You can't silence a carful of Jews with a knife, the way the Captain fixed things for you in Jezzine."

"I'm not interested in silencing anyone," Faisal said quietly, "not even you. Come on."

When they stood under the shadowed arch of the bridge, smelling its heavy odor of damp sandstone and listening to the delicate trickle of water, Faisal hesitated. "I'm going up to take another look at the road," he said, and left Salah under the bridge alone. He climbed to the top of the embankment and took up a position under cover of the sandy ledge where he had a clear view of the entire stretch of the road, both toward Beit Shal and in the direction the Jeep had gone. Relaxing somewhat, satisfied now that he could see anything that approached, he lay down in his own ambush. For the first time that night it was he who had the advantage of the moonlight. He felt a deep envy of the Jewish sentries at Beit Shal, who had only to lie under cover surveying the flat expanse of the plain, waiting for the Fatah squad to show themselves, knowing that with a single round they could bring the whole countryside to their aid. It was the difference between the fox and the hunter, and Faisal felt a deep pleasure at being, however briefly, the hunter. Looking across the bridge, in the direction that he and Salah had come down the ravine, he made out only vague undulations, blurring into a general shadow where the mouth of the valley entered the plain. Remembering Jezzine, he shuddered.

He was shocked to find that for the last several minutes he had forgotten the dead Jew.

The moon was higher now, it stood clear of the orange pall of dust and heat on the jagged horizon. The shadow of the bridge abutments lay at a more acute angle, and in whiter light. Down there, moving with muffled sounds in the creek, Salah was already at work.

"There's nothing to see up there!" he called. "Stop that nonsense, and come down here and help me. There's not going to be anyone else around now. Not after that Jeep; against all known odds. We're as safe under this bridge as if we were in Mecca!"

Reluctantly, Faisal slid down the embankment and crawled into the dark tunnel, lowering his head to avoid imaginary obstructions. At both ends, some thirty feet apart, the low arches formed half circles of moonlight. Salah stood silhouetted in one of these with his hands over his head, working in the dim reflections of the stream. He packed the explosive between the cracks of the stone, working methodically along the top of the arch. Molding each lump of plastic in the palm of his hand, he formed it into a cylinder and wedged it firmly into place, then marked it with one hand while with the other he reached down to retrieve the end of the firing lead. He inserted this into the plastic, spliced the wire, left one end dangling, measured an arm's reach, and began another charge.

"Work from that end," he instructed Faisal, taking command instinctively now that they were engaged in mining. "Use the plastic in that sack, there on the bank." Faisal laid his gun carefully aside and opened the crisp, oiled packets, which rattled under his fingers like picnic wrappers. "Can you see down here?" Salah asked. "Your eyes adjusted yet? All right. There's a pipe running along the underside of the roadbed—here, feel it? Very convenient. It's rusted through, but there are borings in the stones. Must have been angle irons here once." Salah chuckled with satisfaction. "God bless the poor dumb Arabs who built this thing. What lovely cracks and holes they left for us! Make the charges the size of .50-caliber shells," he added more seriously, speaking as if he were lecturing in a classroom. Then, with vengeful pleasure:

"Shove them in deep, as deep as you can get. Pack it in!"

Faisal was already at work, sticking the puttylike, cold, sweating stuff into the hollows that his fingers discovered, probing blindly in the dark, slipping in to explore each crevice in the mortar. The stones were dry. "I want them no more than three feet apart," said Salah. "Hey, student, you hear me? No more than three feet!" Faisal worked intently, hardly listening to Salah. He had other things to worry about. Were their fifteen minutes up already? The Captain would surely have seen the headlights of the car, which had slowed so much when it turned onto the bridge that, from the distance, it might have seemed to have stopped. Would Ali really go on to Beit Shal without them? Faisal wondered how determined he was to adhere to his schedule. But then why else had he kept Hamad with him, and most of the plastic? Salah and he were expendable, even to Ali. Soberly, Faisal realized that while he might distrust the Captain, he did not relish the idea of being stranded this far into Israel with Salah for his only companion.

Salah, meanwhile, was working happily, his boots splashing in the shallow water as he moved from one charge to the next, chatting with a schoolmaster's pleasure in demonstrating a difficult technique. He lectured Faisal. It was, after all, Salah reminded him, a bridge to be mined, it was a serious matter, not to be carelessly rushed, and they would please do it properly.

"For the little bridge's sake," he said, "if not for mine." Deftly he cut the detonating wire, spliced it, and moved three feet toward Faisal to begin another charge. "Poor little Arab bridge, never going to be blown up again. We want to do it justice. Hey, student? You still there?"

"Can't you shut up?" Faisal asked. "Anyone for a mile

around could hear you."

"Tut, tut, the Jew is off chasing smugglers tonight, no doubt arranged by the wily pathans Kassim and Braheim." The smile faded from his voice. Again it became businesslike. "Put the charges in the deepest holes you can find. Pack it between solid stones. We could put two big slugs of the stuff at either end of this tunnel and lift the whole thing fifty feet into the air, but we don't have that much plastic. What we want is a surgical touch, neat, nothing wasted. If we just lay these little balls of mud up here on the surface and fire it, the arch will do exactly what it's supposed to do—it will direct all the force downward, it will throw the blast out the ends of this little tunnel like so much hot air. Oh, I tell you, Faisal, arches are beautiful! Bless the Romans, I have great respect for them. You'd never believe what I've seen a little bridge like this take and not bust! You'd never believe it. Inside the cracks, baby. Deep, deep. We want a shaped charge. Like an antitank shell, armor-piercing. You remember your demolition lessons? They teach you anything but politics up there on Mount Lebanon? All the force of the explosion derived from the compressive shell. Blow up and down, baby, not in and out. Oh, never in and out! Ha, ha! That will do this sweet little bridge so it won't ever have to be done again. Sweet, sad little Arab bridge."

"I remember my lessons," Faisal said, "but if you don't shut up, I'll leave you to do it by yourself." Faisal dreaded this uncontrollable talk, for it reminded him of Salah sitting in his tent, masking his fear of the raid with his irrepressible chatter while Hamad slept and he, Faisal, suffered his humiliating chill. If Salah, the bomber, were that frightened now, under a bridge twelve miles inside

Israel, he preferred not to know it.

Salah laughed, hugely delighted with his anger. "Oh, how I wish we could have mined that drainage culvert at Beit Shal! I was fond of that idea. I especially counted on it. It lent symmetry. A trip wire, a few golf balls of plastic. Along comes the Jew, lickety-split, catch the little Fatahs! Bang! Bang! No more Jew. That had style to it. That was the whole beauty of the raid. After that no Jew would have dared take a step without a mine detector. Now it's just work. Pah!" He spat into the water. "Anyone could do it!"

Faisal moved to the other side of the low arch, bent over to keep his head from hitting the pipe. "Pass me the wires," he said. "I'm ready to fuse."

"Ah, no!" Salah said ironically. He pushed Faisal aside. "Permit me. No offense, but I'll fuse. We've only got one timer and detonator down here. The leads run in series. See? Like this! Tricky, because if one lead misfires the series opens and we get only a partial blast." He began to connect the wires, working silently now, with the concentration of a surgeon performing a delicate operation in total darkness.

"I'm going up, then," said Faisal, relieved to escape the tunnel. Leaving the road unwatched had made him feel as if he were leaving his back exposed. Salah made him apprehensive; the tension which he had sensed in him, the steely-nerved sapper on the outside, the frightened schoolteacher within, his insides rotting with terror, all this suddenly conspired to make Faisal's skin contract with a sense of foreboding. Above all, he needed to believe that the other members of the squad were unafraid, that his own fear was an exaggeration. Yet his talk of a civilian motorcar fooled no one; he knew that it was a

military road, and that anything moving on it was the
Jewish army, not farmers on their way home from playing trik-trak in a Beit Shal tavern. He crouched down
under the embankment, peering toward Beit Shal, his
Sten gun laid before him within easy reach. The dimensionless plain lay like an undulating blanket in the moonlight. Only the winding road was clearly visible, a
ghostly white thread winding across the flank of the hill,
vanishing into obscurity where it dropped down onto
the flatland to reappear where it approached the bridge,
its dusty chalk-white markers advancing out of the darkness in regular order. The road curved sharply on the
foot of the bridge; the macadam was potholed where it
went up over onto the stone roadbed. Faisal understood
then why the Jeep had slowed nearly to a stop before
going on. And Salah, the idiot, had almost opened fire!
Perhaps, Faisal thought, Salah had not imitated the mad
bomber at all, but was himself mad. He strained his eyes
to detect any movement on the road, but the plain was
wrapped in a vague illumination which made him, for a
frightening, vertiginous moment, lose his sense of distance. The veil of silver light seemed then to hang no
more than an inch before his eyes. Thinking with a shudder of the ghostly youth they had left in Jezzine, he
made a brusque movement of his hand, not allowing himself the comfort of actually touching his face, and the
illusion vanished. Far off toward Jezzine he could make
out the faint pinpoints of farm lights, like fireflies danc-
ing on the horizon of a dark, misty beacon, devoid of any
familiar reference of near or far. Unable to visualize
what lay between, Faisal began to slip once more into the
nightmarish sense that the depth of the plain was an illusion, that the moonlight was a screen beyond which he

could see nothing. For a moment the distant lights came to stand an inch before his eyes. Faisal felt himself lost in an alien place. Where were the others? Was it all some horrible dream? There had been a rally for the refugees outside the university gates. He had been in Sarhoud. Was he drunk? Perhaps he would awaken in a moment in his room at the university, to see Aisa reading at the table under a shaded lamp. But in the dream he also saw Aisa floating face down in the Jordan, he heard the snap of green canvas stiffen in the wind like sailcloth, saw, in the narrow beam of a flashlight, a blade of grass, eyes staring, gold-rimmed glasses askew on one ear. He felt haunted by the face of the dying Jew, and turned sharply to look behind him. Atop the distant hill only the radio beacon flashed its red light.

Suddenly Faisal caught a movement to his left—felt it more than actually saw it—a stealthy, sideways disturbance in the uniform blanket of grayness. He turned quickly to face it, but saw nothing. Then he caught another brief advance from the opposite direction, though he could detect it only with his peripheral vision. When he looked directly at it he saw only a veil of moonlight. Feeling a mounting panic, Faisal twisted around, snatched up his Sten gun, and looked frantically in every direction, down the road, back up the ravine, across the plain behind him, wondering how many other shapes were converging upon him, hardly daring to think of Jezzine. If they moved again, he thought, wanting to shout for Salah to help him, he would open fire!

Then from the bottom of the ravine, directly below him, he heard a whisper:

"Faisal, it is I—Ali."

The Captain stepped instantly out into the moonlight,

materializing as startlingly as if he had tunneled up out of the sand. A moment later Hamad appeared from the opposite direction, moving up out of a hollow depression which the moonlight had concealed, shadowed and apparently level, his large field pack giving him the appearance of a hunchback advancing through a fog.

Faisal dropped down under cover of the embankment, resting his gun across his knees, feeling sick with relief. "I saw you coming," he lied. "I wasn't going to fire."

Trembling, he wondered how many more seconds could have passed before he would have blazed away into the moonlight out of sheer panic, not of Jewish infantry, but of a superstitious dread of the youth buried in the ditch, thinly covered with branches. A moment before he had imagined that he commanded a clear view of the approaches to the bridge. Now he realized with a shudder how vulnerable he had been. The wan, silvery light was a fraud. A man could stand fifty feet away and be totally invisible if he didn't move. Looking straight at him, you saw nothing but the general fuzziness of that dusty veil of light. And when he chose to move, it was too late. So it was still the guerrilla squad, Faisal reflected, and not the Jewish sentries who awaited them at Beit Shal, who would have the advantage. He told himself to forget the dead body left in the hedgerow in Jezzine.

"We saw the headlights," Ali said. "We thought you might be in trouble. We divided, crossed the road, and came in from two directions. The danger," he admitted, "was that you would open fire."

Faisal felt instantly ashamed of the doubts he had entertained about the Captain. He replied more effusively than was necessary. "It was nothing, just a civilian motorcar. Salah thought it might have been a Jeep. If it was an army patrol, they didn't spot us."

"All right. The two of you have used your heads. And the mines?"

"Salah's almost finished."

"Good."

Ali seemed to relax, as if he, too, had been plagued by the uncertainty of the moonlight. Not knowing what to expect when they approached the bridge, afraid of what they might find, he had nevertheless come loyally to the aid of his sappers. "We'll pick up the time we've lost by cutting directly across the plain. In this miserable light, you can't see a thing. Anyway," he added, "if the Jew isn't totally asleep, he'll have an outpost watching the spot where this creekbed enters Beit Shal. We'll try to disappoint them."

"Does the bridge still go at 0215?"

"Yes, nothing has changed. Salah has set the timers?"

"He's doing it now."

"Good." Ali disappeared under the bridge. A moment later he and Salah emerged, Salah muttering ". . . battery wired under the pipe we found. Very thoughtful of them to leave it. Nobody could find the stuff, but I couldn't see a thing setting the wires, either."

Ali kept silent, recognizing this complaint for a boast. He knew that if Salah had any doubts about the reliability of his mine he would have kept it to himself. "We'll relieve Hamad of the plastic now," Ali said. They divided the explosives according to their needs; Salah took half, the Captain, who would mine the towers with him, the other half, leaving Faisal and Hamad with empty packs and the now useless C-4 to guard the approaches of the towers while they did their work. The Captain adjusted his pack with a creaking of straps and started off at once across the plain. The squad moved behind him into the dissolving haze of moonlight. He led them straight toward the flank of the nearest hill, beyond which the radio beacon flashed. After a quarter of a mile Faisal looked back, to find the bridge reduced to a dark smudge in a shadowed hollow, while the road, so chalky white before, had been swallowed up entirely in that deceptive pallor which he had mistaken for solid fields of stone and sand. Comforted, Faisal felt secure in his invisibility, as if he might walk with the impunity of a ghost past the first sentry at Beit Shal. His confidence in their chances of survival rose. Reunited with Ali, he regarded the squad with a new feeling of solidarity. And they had had luck, they had had truly incredible luck. All that remained now were the towers, and the Captain and Salah would attend to that. Then they could turn their faces toward the Jordan. Faisal ignored his fatigue, and the dull, nagging shame over what had happened in Jezzine (for that, too, was hardly real now, left on the other side of the invisible plain), and his terror when the dim humped figures of Ali and Hamad, that momentary nightmare of a Jewish patrol, had converged on him at the bridge. He looked up at the hill where now he could begin to make out the first electrical towers marching over its crest like toy soldiers in the moonlight, and visualized what remained to be accomplished, the lyrical, swiftly flowering explosion that would lift them gracefully skyward, tear them methodically to pieces, to fall back with a relieving groan into the deep, smoldering red hole in the earth, and then his familiar tent once again at El Husn, the breakfast line in sunlight, an azure sky, whole days before he would have to cross the Jordan again, days, perhaps even weeks, in which to live.

One Kind of War

THIRTY minutes later the guerrilla squad came over the flank of the hill and entered a gloomy little olive grove. They moved quietly through the grove, smelling the sweet, rotting oil of the trees, until Ali signaled a halt. Once again the road from Jezzine had intercepted them, emerging white and dusty from the moonlit plain to wind around the foot of the hill into Beit Shal. A line of poplars, ascending the base of the hill, cast their shadows across the road. Below them, down a terraced slope, almost three hours to the minute from their crossing the river, they saw the flat roofs of Beit Shal, where a few lighted windows, still burning at midnight, and the pale orange glow of street lamps disclosed a peacefully sleeping town, as any town ought to be, on a moonlit night, in Israel. It was an inviting, open target, its Levantine, domestic slumber as vulnerable as an eighteenth-century village. The first rooftops appeared directly beneath the orchard, where they joined the narrow alleys that ran down into the square; there the canvas awnings of street

stalls cast their shadows over the gray buildings; beyond
the square, against the opposite hillside, the stucco fronts
of tall houses stood out in the moonlight. Behind them
the terraced olive groves commenced once more, ascending into darkness. A motor scooter sputtered across the
town from the west and turned into an alley. In the
square a lone figure moved from door to door, shining a
flashlight across shuttered shop fronts.

"The constabulary," said Ali.

He pointed in the opposite direction, toward a blaze of
lights at the foot of the adjacent hill, separated from their
grove by the steep pass where the Jezzine road entered
Beit Shal.

"The generating station," he said.

It was a large concrete blockhouse, perhaps a hundred
feet on a side and nearly half as tall, situated a mile north
of the town, its massive, gray bulk standing in squat,
powerful contrast to the fragile stucco houses and winding lanes that descended from the nearby slopes, merg-
ing, from several directions, to form the nucleus of Beit
Shal. The fortresslike blockhouse was surrounded by a
high cyclone fence topped with barbed wire. Around the
station area stood tall mercury vapor lamps, their eerie
blue light interdicting a wide zone, perhaps two hundred
yards deep, where anything that might have provided
cover, a stone, tree, or hedge, had been removed and the
ground plowed level. Around that was another, lower
fence with warning signs. "A mine field," Ali commented dryly. "We hadn't known about that." If they
had carried in mortars they might have dropped a few
rounds into the station area from their position high in
the olive grove, but even the 81-mm would not have penetrated the concrete walls. The raid would have sacrificed

itself for nothing. Only the direct hit of a two-thousand-pound aerial bomb could have damaged the station. The generators themselves would be buried even further under additional tons of steel-reinforced concrete. With a cold awareness of their impotence against such an installation, the squad of Fatah crouched in the shadows of the gnarled trees, absorbing, each in his own way, the absurdity of the target which Kassim had assigned them. The militia garrison stood on the outskirts of the zone of lights, beyond the mine field—two barracks, a motor pool, and supply depot, where sentries paced outside the gates.

"Look at that," Salah mused. "Now would you just *look* at that!"

"There will be electrified fences there," Hamad whispered, his voice full of religious dread. "I saw a man touch such a fence one night in the Negev. Another tried to pull him off, and died. We had to leave them both together. I will always remember the way they smelled."

"Pity you didn't try, too," growled Salah.

Astonished, Faisal turned to the Captain. "Major Kassim must be crazy! We wouldn't have had a chance against that station."

"The station doesn't matter," Ali said. "We're not going near it. There are better ways of knocking out the generators than hitting that blockhouse."

With a moment's reflection, Faisal understood the note of grim satisfaction in the Captain's voice. Had Kassim sent them against those lighted fences, across that mine field, so that their deaths would make terror headlines in Tel Aviv and Jerusalem? Very well, they were having none of it.

"Take out the transmission towers," said Ali, "and the

station is useless. When those lines are down we'll have snapped out the lights in every house in the district. They think that generating station is impregnable; we're going to show them that they're wrong. The Jew has become too heavily armored," he added with grim pleasure. "He's like the extinct reptiles. We'll give him a warning this time, and let him sleep on it, if he can." He shifted his weight to peer up toward the hill with the radio beacon. "Now, we have two hours before the moon reaches the west side of the hill. It's black as pitch up there."

The shadow of the hill reached to the foot of the town, where the road turned north, went past the brilliantly lit electrical station, and was lost in darkness. Looking at it, Faisal had a giddy, exhilarating awareness that westward, eighty or ninety miles across other hills and valleys, lay Haifa, and the sea, the ultimate goal. He felt a longing for the Mediterranean that surprised him, a powerful racial need to see minarets standing against that blue horizon once more. Reluctantly, he turned his attention back to the station. From the rear of the blockhouse the first high-voltage lines climbed a complex of transmission towers within the guarded fences, then left the zone of lights and sentries, marching up into the darkness toward the radio beacon.

"Are there patrols on the hill?" asked Salah.

"We won't know until we get up there," replied Ali. "Probably there will be one or two guards, but it's a long way up, and if they patrol the other side, too, we may be able to avoid them. Faisal, you and Hamad cover us. Stay away from the towers; keep above or below wherever we're working. If you see a guard coming up the line you'll have your job to do. Only do it quietly! If any alarm is given we change the detonators to go off in five minutes. In which case," he added, "none of us will get over that hill alive."

"We'll be quiet,'" Faisal heard himself say, though immediately he felt the absurdity, the hopeless inadequacy of any reply he might have made to a proposition to stalk from behind, to kill silently with a knife. He felt a solid, physical dread of such an encounter. He would do his job, of that he was sure (he would never hesitate again, not as he had in Jezzine!), though to take a life "quietly," as the Captain put it, left him feeling nauseous.

Salah and Ali moved cautiously down the slope of the olive terraces. The ledges were walled with unmortared stones, Arab terraces, perhaps a century old, and they crumbled under their weight. With each rattle of stones the squad hesitated for a moment, listening, then went on, Faisal and Hamad bringing up the rear. When they had dropped out of sight of Beit Shal they found the Jezzine road still between them and the hill with the towers; looking down toward the road Faisal saw the drainage culvert which Salah had first noted on the map. It was a black, dripping hole, perhaps a meter in diameter, passing under the roadbed where the creek, also flowing in through the narrow pass from the plain, was reduced to a trickle in the bottom of a rock-choked ravine. The culvert looked ominous, and he was glad to be going on without mining it. The only shelter there was the obscurity of the overhanging bank, and the shadows of the trees across the road. Beyond it, the opposite hill rose into darkness.

The Captain and Salah crossed the road one at a time, taking what cover they could from the trees, and vanished up the hillside. Faisal signaled for Hamad to cross ahead of him. But Hamad was mesmerized by the tunnel he was supposed to have mined. He stared down at its gaping mouth. "Go," Faisal ordered, "go!" Reluctantly, Hamad went down past the open end of the pipe. When he was safely over, Faisal took one final look in both directions, turned to glance back up toward the orchard, and went down into the creekbed, splashed through the shallow water, climbed up past the drainage culvert, and crossed the road at a dead run. He found the others waiting at the base of a gulley that led up the hill.

For the first time nothing stood between them and their goal but darkness.

"You all right?" Ali asked.

"Yes."

"What's the matter with the mule?" Salah shook him roughly. "He's moaning like an old woman."

Hamad suppressed a groan. "Nothing," he whispered, "it's nothing. . . ." He crouched beside Faisal, who heard the delicate clicking of the Druze beads through his fingers. With a numbed mutter, Hamad said, "Don't worry . . . the road." Then, ardently, "It's over—it's over now!"

Faisal looked at him, puzzled, until Ali pointed toward the electrical station.

"We'll climb to the left," he said. "Stay low, or you'll make fine targets. And keep an eye on the downhill slope. If there's anyone there, he'll have us against the moonlight. Uphill of us they won't see a thing, we'll see them."

Salah was already moving off, getting as far away from Hamad as he could, picking his way between boulders and ledges of stone. The terrain was rugged. The entire hill seemed made of loose stones. The smallest were the size of loaves of bread, and slipped treacherously; the largest were solid shoulders of massive rock, eroded and smooth as marble. The squad moved slowly, taking diverse paths around the boulders that obstructed their way, winding upward through a labyrinth, to meet and go on together across the ledges of shale and dry turf. Hamad stayed close to Faisal, dogging his steps as he had when they crossed the river, so that again Faisal had the uncomfortable feeling that if he stopped Hamad would collide with him.

Soon, off to the south, their climbing again raised the lights of Beit Shal. Ahead the sky was aglow from the generating station. Fifteen minutes later they were looking down at it from an elevation of several hundred feet. They advanced cautiously toward the line of transmission towers. Invisible from the olive grove, the towers were now clearly silhouetted against the starry sky. Each was a triangular frame, some seventy feet high, with double sets of outstretched arms that lifted the cables over the hill. The lines sagged out of view, lost under the dark horizon of the hillside, to merge again heavily, as if from the bottom of the sea, to meet the waiting arms of the next tower. For several minutes Ali remained perfectly still, watching intently for some sign of patrols along the line. The squad heard, and saw, nothing. Only the distant, muted waterfall rumble of the generators disturbed the absolute stillness of the night.

"Come on," muttered Ali, "let's have a look at one of them."

The Captain and Salah vanished into the darkness. Faisal knelt down with his Sten gun ready, peering ahead at the line of towers. As soon as Ali was gone his imagination took full rein. What if the Jewish sentries came in behind them? Would they be able to see them if they

came down the hill? Were they already under surveil-
lance, a Jewish sentry in a hidden bunker nearby whis-
pering their position into a radiophone? But these were
only a few of the imponderables. There were too many
to worry about, and Faisal waited tensely, focusing his
attention on the direction the Captain and Salah had
taken. When Ali returned he was alone.

"We've had luck. There are no fences around the towers, but they've quarried rock up ahead, so watch out for
the holes." The Captain knelt beside them, speaking with
more enthusiasm than Faisal had yet heard him, as if even
he thought that the raid now had a chance of success.
"The towers are balanced on structural points as thin as
pencils. It's all aluminum, very modern and advanced. It
will be like knocking over toys."

Faisal looked up toward the top of the hill, where the
towers marched over the crest into the moonlight. "Will
you work upward?" he asked.

"Yes. We want four towers, to make sure the cables
snap. We'll take out more if we have time." He checked
his watch. "We've still got sunrise to worry about. I'll
give us fifty minutes on the hill. Salah's already at work
on the tower directly ahead. You and Hamad stay below
us, where you can see anyone coming up the line in the
lights of the station. If they come down, you'll have
them silhouetted against the ridge. But for God's sake,
keep yourselves low, and stay out of sight! We won't be
able to look out for ourselves under the towers. You're
all the support we've got. And remember, the Jew
doesn't need to worry about a little noise; he'll open fire
at once if he thinks there's any danger. Take him from
behind, at the throat if you can, and be quick about it."

"Yes," said Faisal.

Still the Captain hesitated. "Well . . . all right, then."

"Captain Ali," Faisal said with an effort, humiliated, remembering Jezzine, "Ali, don't worry. I'll do it this time!"

"I'm not worried." Faisal felt Ali's strong fingers grip his arm. He was given a rough, peremptory shake. "We'll meet you at the bottom on the other side. Then it's Jezzine, and home free. Hamdullah! Praise Allah, we've hurt the Jew tonight. This time he'll feel it. Good luck."

"Good luck," Faisal said. He watched Ali move away into the darkness, then turned to Hamad, who squatted behind him, his head lowered, as if studying the darkness between his feet, listening to the clicking of his prayer beads.

"Stay back, and cover me," he whispered. "Let's go."

Hamad, holding his Sten gun in one hand, raised his head suddenly. "Now?" Absently, his meditation broken, he jerked the bolt back with a loud snap.

Faisal spun around angrily. "Not your gun!" he said. "Didn't you hear the Captain?"

Hamad grunted indifferently. "I heard him."

"Keep behind me then," Faisal said, and started out. At that moment he could think of a dozen men he would rather have had with him than Hamad. The footing was treacherous; though he moved cautiously, Faisal's boots sent stones clattering down the slope. The Fatah squad depended upon one another now as absolutely as alpinists strung out across a vertical cliff, and traversing that dark and unknown place Faisal was not reassured to have the Druze fanatic at his back. Would he do his job? Could he, of all men, be expected to resist Fate? Or would he regard the Jewish sentries as the hand of God, and rush to meet them?

Faisal reached the first dark holes of the quarry, and took up a position behind a large block of cut stone where he could cover the approaches of the transmission line. He told himself not to worry about Hamad. There were more important things to see to. He focused his attention on his job: laid his Sten gun before him on the rough surface of the block of stone; checked his ammunition clips; reached down, his hand trembling slightly with involuntary distaste, to make sure that his knife handle was free. But when he turned to see if Hamad had kept his proper distance he saw with a jolt that a dark figure sat behind him, within arm's reach, watching his every movement, his legs dangling over the edge of the hole, as motionless and as silent as the stones.

It was Hamad, who looked down at him with the patience of an owl. Angrily, Faisal pulled him down into the hole.

"Are you crazy? I told you to stay back!" He controlled a desire to strike him in the face. "What good can two of us do here?"

"It doesn't matter," Hamal replied. "Not any more." Again Faisal heard the precise ticking of the Druze beads, dropping one at a time through Hamad's fingers with the mechanical rhythm of a clock. "All that is beside the point."

Faisal looked at him sharply. "What do you mean?"

Hamad shrugged. His voice was almost ironic, a tone as alarming in Hamad as if one of the stones of the crater had sat upright and begun to speak. "If I am behind you and a Jew comes—you see? It is hopeless. You die if I don't shoot. If I shoot the Jew dies, but then all the Jews come, and you still die." He added quietly, "We are all dying. We are always dying."

"Use your knife!" Faisal said.

"You misunderstand me. Of course I will use my knife," Hamad replied philosophically, "if there is time."

"You came up here to tell me that?" Faisal asked incredulously.

"I had no choice," said Hamad. He continued to stare at him fixedly, as if waiting. "But it is all beside the point now."

Faisal was irritated and puzzled. All night the Syrian had been mulish and silent. The only ten consecutive words he had spoken had been to tell Salah that he had lost equipment in the river. Now to have him offer his laconic comment on the hopelessness of their situation, trapped on a hill fifteen miles inside Israel, filled Faisal with an irrational foreboding. He preferred Hamad not to think at all, or at least, if he had to think, to keep it to himself, for in that Druze mind only lurid and alarming forms took shape. With Hamad beside him in the cavity of the stone quarry, Faisal was not cheered to find that in fact the fanatic had been thinking, perhaps ruminating all night about the raid, and was prepared, on the hill above Beit Shal, to declare it hopeless. Hamad had offered a pronouncement, not a speculation. And could he, Faisal, argue with it? What were their chances if they were seen? It was they who were vulnerable now, not the Jew. They had given up their mobility to accomplish their work on the towers. Even if they came upon a sentry from behind, what real chance did they have of killing him with a knife before he could cry out or squeeze off a round from his carbine? One shot, and the whole garrison would come to life. They would swarm up the hill. Faisal shuddered. There was something welling up within the Syrian, a slow, ominous threat of some absurd revelation, a look on his face, as of a mountain straining to bring forth an idea, which Faisal had not seen since that first night on Mount Lebanon. Hamad, once set in motion, would be as impossible to stop as an avalanche. Faisal decided to keep him with him.

"All right, we'll stay together then," he said. "'When the Captain and Salah begin work on the next tower we'll move up through the quarry." He spoke slowly, as if to a frightened child, though his mind hovered else-where over the abyss where Hamad could plunge them all if he chose. "We'll keep a little below them all the way up. If sentries come on their rounds, they ought to walk the line." Grimly, he added, "I'll take the first; if there's a second he'll be yours."

"But it's already too late for that," Hamad said, squat-ting behind him on his heels, in abject, peasant fashion, his arms extended over his knees. "All that is useless."

Faisal's instinct was not to reply, to ignore him as one would a willful child, but his impatience with Hamad overcame his caution, for here was the cryptic utterance of an idiot; it was exactly that Mount Lebanon sense that here spoke an inspired fool that rendered the comment too unnerving to let pass without challenge.

"This is no time to lose your nerve," he said. "It won't be too late until we make a mistake. Watch up the line. They'll be finished with that tower soon."

But Hamad did not look up; he seemed hardly to hear. He stared straight ahead without stirring, as if he were listening to other voices, with arms still dangling over his knees in a helpless gesture of resignation, waiting; some-thing—it was impossible to say what—moved in the dark corridors of that mind. In his outstretched hands the beads continued to tick.

"We are dead," he murmured. *"I know."*

Everything about the Syrian now filled Faisal with dread. He wondered by what tormented process of thought he had reached the conclusion, which was echoed by a rising, primitive voice within Faisal himself that, caught in the dark hollows and ledges of the stone quarry, they were already lost—indeed, had been lost since they entered Israel.

"You're not making sense," Faisal said levelly, trying manfully to resist the intuition that everything was falling apart. "What are you talking about?"

"The culvert."

"What culvert?"

Hamad stared at the dark ledge of stone before him, still waiting, shaking his head slowly at some hopeless absurdity which none but he could understand, a fatal irony which only he could fully appreciate.

"The detonator," he whispered. "I have it. I have always had it. It has been with me from the beginning. It has been with me since the day I was born." The beads ticked furiously; he lifted his face heavenward, for the first time lamenting in a passionate voice. "Oh, *Ah*lah! *Ah*lah Akbar! How I have tried to keep it away, and how it is with me now! And I have been weak. And I have sinned. *Ah*lah be praised in His mercy . . . in His mercy!"

The exquisite thrill of dread which Faisal then felt could have been no purer if Hamad had produced a hooded cobra from a basket. An involuntary shudder ran down his spine. It was as if Hamad's words had released a premonition of disaster which he had carried with him from the East Bank of the Jordan, had carried with him, perhaps, from the first day he could remember in the refugee camps of Sidon—the closed walls, the fences, the limits of existence. He had thought the enemy was the Jew, and the darkness of Israel; now the enemy was sitting beside him, wearing the outfit of a Fatah commando; the enemy was superstition, and dread, and centuries of sloth, and its name was Hamad. The enemy was Fate. Something within Faisal wanted to cry out, *Yes, it was all too easy! He had known the worst would be last!* A racial hopelessness, a deep and abiding wisdom of defeat, made him want to give up at once with a moan of despair, sink down into the hole, and let the raid fulfill its destiny without him. *I knew! I knew!* He thought that he heard overhead the distant sound of steel doors clanging shut, the howling of a dog far off in Jezzine. But all this was merely the effect of fatigue, the danger of their position, his impatience with Hamad's stupidity. Manfully, he fought his panic down. He determined that next morning, resting in his tent at El Husn, he would not have to look back with shame to this scene in the craters of the stone quarry where he had surrendered his reason to a childish terror.

"The detonator," he said quietly. "Do you mean the one you lost in the river?"

"I did not lose it," Hamad answered, glancing at him with a furtive, hopeful look, as if in that single exchange of glances Faisal would comprehend everything. *You knew! Yes, you knew!* But after a moment he lowered his eyes and drew himself back into his crouch, studying the stones again with a groan of despair, lamenting his own weakness. Had the eyes, for an unguarded second, cried out for help? The groan, ending in a bitter laugh, admitted that no help was possible. With a great effort, he said:

"I tried to lose it . . . but I could *not*."

"What the devil do you mean," Faisal asked impatiently, "you tried to lose it?"

"What I said—I tried to drop it in the river. But I was prevented." He whispered with suppressed passion, "Oh, I have always been prevented! I see that now."

"Prevented?"

Hamad struggled for words. He clenched his fists and drew them up before his face, as if when he opened them a strange bird might fly out. "All my life I have waited for this," he said gloomily. "Oh, how clear it all is at last! But I did not expect . . ." He looked speechlessly at Faisal, his eyes widening, then up at the stars. "Who would have thought it ends like this? It was God—something. *Some*thing. Always ahead of me. Always behind me. Always there! Ah, I can't explain it—not to you!"

"But why did you tell Salah that you had lost the detonator?"

Hamad stared at him blankly. "I was afraid."

"But afraid of what?" Faisal asked with vexation. He glanced up at the transmission lines. When he looked back at Hamad he found him staring at him with the same transfixed expression, as if he saw his reflection in stone. "Afraid of *what?*" he demanded.

Hamad opened his mouth, closed it, opened it again. He drew his fists up once more, clenching them as if to squeeze out the word that would make everything plain. His need to explain himself was more than he could bear. Then, as if suddenly realizing that Faisal had not understood the simplest part of it, he said almost gently, almost forgivingly:

"Why, I was afraid of death."

Faisal stared at him incredulously.

"I will die on the road," Hamad explained. "In the mine. That was why I tried to throw away the detonator. I could not throw away the mine," he said reasonably, "because you would have heard it splash in the river. But of course it was all useless. All of it."

At last Faisal understood. So it was this that Hamad suffered all the way into Israel! Against such a fear his own fretful worry over ambushes and militiamen seemed trivial. But could even Hamad, in his demented imagination, actually think that he was fated to die if he mined the drainage tunnel? Appalled, yet fascinated, Faisal tried to imagine the quality of such fear, the despondency a man must feel who was stalked, not by men, but by God. He looked at Hamad's face, but saw only a mask. How long had he "known"? Since that afternoon, when he, the messenger of Fate, had kicked his cot to tell him that they were going with Captain Ali? For the last month? Faisal shuddered with disgust, but also with pity. Yet now that he understood what was troubling Hamad he knew even less what to do about it.

"Well," he said at last, turning calmly to peer up the slope of the stone quarry, as if he might exorcise this nightmare by disregarding it, "you tricked Fate this time, only don't let Salah know that you have that detonator. You'd better throw it away."

"But you see, I cannot," Hamad protested.

"Toss it away," Faisal said quietly, watching him with growing fear. "That's all you have to do, and everything will be all right. We're across the road, and nothing has happened. Don't you see? It's behind us. I'm certainly not going to tell Ali. Why did you keep the detonator, anyway? Just throw it away."

Hamad shook his head helplessly. "Don't you think I've tried? Every time we stopped to rest I tried to leave it behind. But I couldn't do it. I was prevented. I am only allowed to talk to you because it is not yet time! When it is time, I will go."

"That's crazy," Faisal replied. "You can throw it away if you want to. All you mean by 'prevented' is that you didn't want to. Give it to me and I'll do it."

Hamad stared at him as if he were mad. "You cannot do it either. It is no use trying."

Faisal looked anxiously up at the transmission lines. Captain Ali and Salah had already moved to the next tower; he saw their cautious advance where they were silhouetted, once or twice, against the sky. Ignoring Hamad's words, he reached for his Sten gun and prepared to crawl upward through the quarry. "Come on, they're at the second tower. We've got to move up. Deep behind me, and for God's sake, be quiet!"

"I cannot," Hamad replied. "Don't you see that? I can't go with you any more."

Faisal stopped at the top of the ledge. Hamad had not moved. He hesitated for a moment, looking up at the towers, then slid back into the hole, feeling the same deep chill that had followed him while he wandered through the camp that afternoon, waiting for nightfall, as if it were his own fate, not Hamad's, that he was struggling against. "What do you mean, you can't go? Ali and Salah are counting on us!"

"I cannot go with you," Hamad said stubbornly. "I have already come too far." He stared at the bottom of the hole. The prayer beads began to tick again. Then, emphatically, "I must go down to mine the road now."

Faisal drew himself together with an effort, as if he were resisting the weightless substance of a dream. He sat down beside Hamad, prepared to reason. "Look, if Ali finds out . . ."

"What does Ali matter to me?" Hamad asked indig-
nantly. "I am already dead! Don't you think I would
come with you if I could? Don't you see that I have
tried? I am only a man, like you. All night I have run
from my fate, but it is still with me. I am not allowed to
go to the top of the hill with you. You are welcome to
live—I, I must mine the road!" He looked beseechingly
at Faisal. "Don't you feel it? You, too, are prevented."
Sadly, he concluded, "We are always, everywhere prevented."

Faisal forgot Ali and Salah. Until he did something to
quiet him, Hamad was their greatest danger. If the
Syrian were truly mad he would have to stop him.

"You should have thrown the mine away," he said
angrily, "not the detonator."

Hamad shrugged. "I could not. You saw that Salah
would not let me. He was—"

"Yes, yes, I know." Faisal interrupted, wanting to
cover his ears in order to think. "He was *prevented*. Just
be quiet!"

Hamad fell silent, waiting. Even the constant ticking
of the beads stopped while Faisal tried urgently to foresee what lay ahead. He weighed the alternatives, feeling
as though he were sitting beside a ticking bomb. He
could not physically prevent Hamad from returning to
the Jezzine road. The Syrian had the strength of three
men; not even Ali could have brought him down. It was
no use reasoning with him, for now he regarded him as
finally and wholly mad. He realized that the greatest mistake of the raid had not been the close timing, the impossible distance, or the audacity of striking at Beit Shal—
the greatest mistake, perhaps the fatal one, had been to

suppose that they could use Hamad for a beast of burden without entangling themselves with his gods, his super-stitions, his dreamy narcissism, finally, with his own fate. In the end, Faisal thought, they should have known that Hamad would be irresponsible. And Faisal was his tent mate. It had been his mistake.

As a last resort he could let him go down to mine the road, allow him to play out the dark necessity of his nightmare. After all, they had intended to mine the road; only Hamad's lie had changed the plan. What else was the mine for? Faisal, looking at it reasonably, saw it as the least dangerous path.

For a final moment his resentment swelled up within him. "What are we going to do about Captain Ali and Salah?" he asked, turning to Hamad.

"Like us, they are in God's hands," replied Hamad. Then, with steadfast faith: "The Jew cannot touch them if it is not ordained."

"And if it is ordained?" Faisal asked bitterly, though his sarcasm was tinged with an unadmitted fear.

"Then nothing can help them."

Faisal looked up at the spidery towers that stood out against the faintly starry sky, cursing inwardly. He wanted desperately to escape that hole where he was im-prisoned with the Druze fanatic, who had chosen this night, of all nights, to toy with his fatal dreams. But Faisal, too, had known that it was coming. Yes, yes, he thought, he had known! He had felt it. All he could do now was combat it, and try to get both of them to the other side of that hill alive.

What would the Captain have done? They could say that Hamad had found the detonator after all. Would Ali still want the culvert mined? Or would he tell him to cut

Hamad's throat, suddenly and noiselessly, and so put an end to the nuisance? He sat with him now in the hole, like a racial curse, a legacy of the past. What was such a man doing in Fatah? Quietly, uncertain whom to blame, he cursed the Major.

Quickly then, Faisal made his decision. When he glanced at Hamad he found him fingering a final glass bead, his face transfigured with the holy zeal of martyrs.

"Let me see the detonator."

Hamad unzipped the leg pocket of his jump suit and produced it, still sealed in its oiled wrapper.

"Is it dry?"

"It was never in the water."

"And the C-4?"

"Oh, yes," Hamad nodded, "in my pack. Also very dry."

Faisal took a deep breath. "All right, you go down to the road. Now listen to me, Hamad—you will mine the culvert exactly as Captain Ali ordered. Nothing is going to happen down there. All that is crazy. You'll set the mine and meet us at the bottom of the hill. We'll come down north of the radio tower." He shook him roughly, trying to excite a spark of reason in his dazed eyes. "Do you understand? North of the tower."

"I will do what I must."

Fascinated in spite of himself, Faisal could not keep from asking, "What did you think was going to happen down there?"

"I don't know."

"But you said . . ."

"I see nothing," answered Hamad, turning to put the detonator back into his leg pocket. He adjusted the weight of his pack. "Beyond the road, I see nothing. All my life I have known what lay just ahead. Now for the first time I see nothing."

So this was all it was? Faisal felt a moment's disappointment, and a bitter contempt for the stuff of superstition, made always of such empty fears. He recoiled from his own curiosity. Hamad was no better than a child, justly frightened, perhaps, but of nothing more substantial than a child's dream. Who could not, if he chose, paralyze his will by believing that Death awaited him around the next corner? And like a willful child, Faisal thought resentfully, Hamad would have his way.

"We all feel like that tonight," he said, "even Captain Ali. No one thinks of what lies ahead; we all see 'nothing' until we get out of this alive. Forget it. Do your job. Ali and Salah are doing theirs. It shouldn't take you more than thirty minutes on the road."

Hamad was silent.

"You know how to set the C-4? In that drainage pipe you ought to be able to fix it to the bottom of the road-bed. Only the firing pin has got to be lined up with the angle of maximum thrust—straight up under the weight of the trigger."

"I know the C-4," answered Hamad. "It will go off."

Faisal was impatient to get him off the hill and away from the towers. "All right," he said. "Go on, then. Go on!"

Hamad turned his back without another word and crawled out of the hole. Faisal watched him make his way down through the stone quarry, then around the lower flank of the hill toward the Jezzine road. Turning abruptly, he looked down at the generating station. It was like looking into a searchlight. It took his eyes a moment to recover before he could once more make out the dark, angular shapes of the stone quarry, which extended beyond the line of towers, and for an indefinite distance above him. Farther up, the crest of the hill was already edged with moonlight. The radio beacon continued to flash—two red, followed by a long white, then again two reds. For the first time Faisal found himself alone. The threatening presence of Israel closed around him in the darkness. He allowed his right hand to inch forward until it touched the reassuring solidity of his Sten gun. He wanted desperately to tell Ali what he had done, but then he would leave them unprotected. He knew what Ali's reply would be.

Why are you telling me this? It was your responsibility. Get back to your position!

The Captain and Salah were finished with the second tower. Faisal moved cautiously up through the dark quarry, keeping a lookout for sentries along the line, until he was a little above them. Below, across the intervening darkness, he could see the lighted garrison barracks. The small figures of two guards walked across the compound yard toward the motor pool. One of them had a flashlight. There were no sentries visible at the gates, yet anyone moving up the line would be silhouetted in that light, a perfect target. Regretfully, Faisal reminded himself that he must not use his gun. He wondered how close a man would have to approach before you could use a knife. A meter? A foot? If it happened, Faisal thought, he would stay under cover until the last moment; but he would not surrender the advantage of the hill. If the Jew came up from the garrison, he would attack him frontally, rising up before him too quickly for alarm. If he came down the hill it would be easier—he could let him pass, then take him from behind. These arrangements made, he relaxed somewhat, feeling unreal, as if he were a character in the cinema. He kept his hand away from the repulsive handle of the knife.

From his higher position in the run of the quarry he could now look down toward the road. It was visible in the avenue of moonlight that streamed through the narrow pass between the hills. Hamad was no longer in sight. Relieved, Faisal concluded that he had reached the drainage tunnel. Then he saw him emerge from the pipe, go down to the bottom of the gulley to carry something back with him (the mine? Faisal wondered) and disappeared again.

Faisal felt the burden of irrational fear lifted from his shoulders now that Hamad was at work. All night they had had luck, truly incredible luck. It would hold. The C-4 was their insurance; it would prevent anything from crossing the road. If the Captain and Salah contented themselves with only four towers, they would be over the hill at the same time that Hamad finished laying his mine.

Faisal crawled somewhat higher through the ledges and overturned blocks of the quarry, instinctively pressing closer to the crest of the hill, closer to freedom, and waited tensely. He was only a few dozen yards from the transmission towers; a dull, pulsing hum came from a nearby transformer. Faisal could not see it but he imagined a high cyclone fence, and the deadly sign, "Danger —High Voltage." The very stones of the dark quarry seemed to pulse with electricity. As in a child's dream, Faisal felt that if he put out his hand he would touch a fence and be electrocuted. Above him the high tops of the tower structures were outlines in deeper black on a black and star-speckled sky, like the masts of sailing ships. When he looked up the entire hillside seemed to roll with the wheeling constellations. Faisal crouched deeper in his hole. Momentarily he pictured Major Kassim sitting in the command post, smoking a cigarette under a shaded lamp, waiting through the long night for word from Beit Shal. But this made him feel as if Kassim were watching him (as if he, Faisal Abu Ajran, had become no more than an extension of Kassim's mind), and he stopped thinking about it. He pressed his right shoulder against the comforting solidity of the sandstone. Feeling the dimensions of the hole, he thought of a block the size used in houses, public buildings, and monuments. He looked at the towers, counted the remaining minutes before he would see the Captain and Salah start for the top of the hill. His heart pounded with the agony of waiting. He thought of the relief of putting Beit Shal behind them, of actually facing the Jordan. Now that the beginning of the end was in sight Faisal found that it was harder to endure the waiting. All the desire to live surged back. His nerves were stretched to the breaking point.

Quietly, calming himself, he adjusted the straps of his ammunition belt, and turned to glance down toward the road.

It was then that he saw the headlights. They were still a considerable distance away, perhaps three or four miles out on the plain. But somewhere in that white blanket of moonlight a vehicle was coming toward Beit Shal, heading for the culvert where Hamad was still at work with his mine. In that second of comprehension Faisal felt himself swept toward one of those moments when complex decisions come instantaneously, as if of themselves. As if by genius. As if they were the works of providence.

The vehicle was too far off for Hamad, down under

the road, to hear it. Faisal tried to decide if he should remain where he was, hoping that Hamad would stay out of sight when the vehicle crossed the culvert, the mine disarmed. Or should he leave his post to warn him of the approaching danger? What if the trigger were already set? Would Hamad hear the engine in time? The explosion would alert all of Beit Shal. Ali and Salah would be trapped on the hill. Faisal weighed the risks on both sides, leaving the Captain and Salah unprotected on the slope, or risking the mine being touched off. He was responsible for Hamad's being on the road. Desperately, caught without Ali to tell him what to do, the fate of the others in his hands, Faisal struggled with himself. Then, before he realized that he had reached a decision, he was scrambling up out of the quarry and running down the hillside, leaping over stones, the blood pounding in his head, racing the vehicle for the culvert. He went down the rocky hillside as fast as he could, twisting between the crazed labyrinth of boulders, and broke into the moonlit side of the slope. Dashing wildly downward, recklessly exposing himself, wanting to cry out for help, he stumbled and fell, bloodying himself against the boulders, got up, and went on.

No one moved on the road. Either Hamad was finished with the mine and on his way to the rendezvous, or still in the drainage tunnel.

Faisal hurtled blindly downhill. When he was two hundred yards from the bottom he knew that he was too late. The headlights became a truck, rolling smoothly up the Jezzine road, gaining the culvert before he could possibly reach it.

Faisal threw caution to the winds. "Hamad!" he cried, still racing downward, his arms flung out on both sides like a tightrope walker about to fall from a dizzying height. "Hamad!"

But nothing moved in the culvert.

At a hundred yards the truck became a school bus, rounded the last curve of the plain in clear view, and drove straight for Beit Shal.

"Hamad! Hamad! The mine—"

When Faisal was a few dozen yards from the roadside, scrambling down the last ravine, the bus swept by under him. Its interior lights were on. Through the glowing, dusty windows he saw that it was full of children. The racks atop the bus were piled with the dark shapes of sleeping bags and rolled-up tents. Children, Faisal absurdly thought, returning home from camp. But why at midnight? Why on a military road? He doubled up, wrapped his arms around himself, his stomach in his mouth, and closed his eyes.

"Hamad," he said quietly, "the trigger. Release the trigger. Oh, please, dear God—the trigger."

At that moment Hamad emerged from the pipe. He stood below the roadbed, looking up with stupefied wonder into the headlights of the oncoming bus, and then threw himself headlong into the poplar trees. The last sound that Faisal heard, out of the open rear window of the bus, was the sound of children singing a rondeau. A split second later that living, delicate sound was annihilated by the blast of the mine. The front half of the bus disappeared in a white flash that lit the opposite hillside as far as the olive terraces. The concussion was terrific, but Faisal was too close to hear it. The sound wave struck him with a single, massive blow, knocking him flat and hammering all his senses closed. When he recovered, perhaps a minute later, the shattered remnants of the bus, the rear axle, a portion of the body, and the chassis as far as the middle of its frame lay in the ravine. In the black crater left by the mine a gas tank was burning with the fierce sound of a blowtorch.

Slowly, in the flaring light of the burning gasoline, a handful of children stirred here and there amid the wreckage. Elsewhere bodies and pieces of debris littered the road. A small, thin voice, almost inhuman, began to scream. Dazed, Faisal got to his feet and walked unsteadily to the bottom of the hill.

All over Beit Shal the lights were coming on. At the garrison a klaxon began to ring. A few children, those who could, got to their feet; others were moving, as if experimentally, an arm or leg; most of them lay motionless like bundles of burnt rags amid the carnage of wheels, smoldering tires, and fragments of shattered metal. An eerie silence lay over the scene. Faisal heard only the ringing in his ears. It was like a moment, unreal, from a silent movie. For a hundred yards, as far as the ring of the fire penetrated the darkness, Faisal saw a landscape of smoking seat cushions, lunch pails, arms, intestines, twisted metal pieces of doors and fenders, all of it covered with broken glass and a reflective wet surface, oil or blood or unignited gasoline, as if the entire mess had been sprayed from a hose. On all sides now the survivors were crying. One boy wandered past Faisal, picking his way through the wreckage, as if searching for his possessions. A teacher, mistaking Faisal for a militiaman, stumbled toward him out of the ravine. He advanced lurching up and down with a comic limp.

"The children," he gasped. "For the love of God . . . help them. The children—!"

He collapsed a few paces from Faisal, who then saw

that this apparition's left foot had been blown off. He tried to stand, but fell again.

"Help them . . . help them! For God's sake, can't you see—?"

Faisal wandered off a short distance. His head was ringing with the shock of the explosion; he heard only the high, metallic crash of steel doors slamming shut.

A small girl looked up at him. She clutched the front of her dress, which was dark with blood, and watched him pass. He went down to the ditch, past the driver crushed under the engine block, and peered into the remnants of the bus, where a knot of children huddled together in the rear, afraid to come out. Some of them were weeping with shock. In his mind, Faisal still heard only the slamming of doors.

The small girl had followed him. Still clutching the front of her dress, she reached out her arm, badly lacerated by pieces of shattered glass, to touch Faisal. He did not resist; he scarcely noticed her. She pressed her face against him, looking up at him for comfort. He felt her arms embrace his leg. The child and he were still standing together, surveying the smoldering ruin about them, when the first army Jeeps arrived from Beit Shal.

The militiamen, some of them brothers and fathers of the children on the bus, began to search through the wreckage with flashlights, frantically calling out their names. A roadblock was set up to keep the other citizens of Beit Shal away, although when automobiles arrived with parents of children who had been on the bus they were let through to give first aid. Some of the women were Oriental Jews, who gathered what they could find of their children and began their ritual screaming, tearing their hair, scarring their faces with their fingernails. An officer arrived and began directing the rescue work. A detail was soon scouring the area with a mine detector.

"Captain Metzger, they want you on the radio!"

"All right! Nathan, get those kids out of the bus. You there, George—get those plasma cartons up here!"

A patrol was sent down the road, heavily armed.

"We'll catch the bastards this time," Captain Metzger said, "we'll catch them! Where the devil are the ambulances? Get tourniquets on these kids!"

Through it all Faisal wandered alone, completely ignored, until above them on the hillside four rapid explosions rocked the transmission towers. Three towers slowly collapsed with a groaning crash. A second later the quarry was illuminated by a brilliant flash of blue light as the high-voltage lines parted. Over the flank of the hill the houses of Beit Shal vanished into darkness.

Ali, Faisal thought, staring up at the hill, as if watching from a great distance. Quietly, with a deep sense of release, as if everything were now finished, he repeated, "Ali."

Captain Metzger ran across the road to a Jeep with a radio. "They're on the hill! Do you hear me? They've blown the towers. Get up there! Get up there!"

A machine gun opened up at the base of the hill, near the garrison. The militia patrols moved up toward the quarry under its fire, the flashes of their rifles spreading across the slope. Near the top Faisal saw the muzzle bursts of a lone machine gun answering, and imagined, for a fleeting second, that he saw a dark figure run over the crest of the hill into the moonlight. The fire fight continued, the patrols moving steadily toward the top, until at last the lone machine gun was silenced. Again Faisal thought, with deep sadness, Ali. He next thought of Hamad, who had killed them all, but felt nothing. Then he gazed into the blare of the burning fuel tank, where the flames still rolled up into billowing clouds of black smoke.

Not until the ambulances had arrived and a spotlight was set up to illuminate the scene of the disaster did a young soldier recognize Faisal. He struck him at once in the face with his rifle butt.

"I've got one!" he shouted. "Here, a Fatah! I've got one of them!"

The older militiamen looked up from the stretchers.

A woman's voice screamed, "Kill him!"

Rough hands reached down to drag Faisal into a ditch. Women clawed at his face. Boots and fists struck his head. At last Captain Metzger appeared and the soldiers held the women back.

"Murderer!" they shrieked. "Murderer! Are you going to let him live?"

"David, keep them back," Captain Metzger ordered.

The women fought their husbands to get at Faisal. "Give us our babies, then," they wailed. "Tell him to bring our babies back!"

Captain Metzger took out his .45 and held the muzzle to Faisal's head. "Are there other mines?" he asked.

Faisal said nothing. He heard only the slamming of steel doors, a corridor of echoes.

"Are there other mines!" the Captain demanded. "Tell me, or by God I'll blow your filthy brains out!"

A balding militiaman came across the road. "Captain," he said, "let me have him. For one minute. That's all I ask." He pointed to the wreckage of the bus, where the chassis was blown outward with the cruel shape of a steel flower. "My kid is over there, what's left of her. Go take a look, Captain."

"Is it Rachel?" he asked.

The militiaman nodded. "Rachel. Just give me one minute with him."

Captain Metzger lowered his .45. "We've got to have a prisoner," he said.

"But they've got another."

"Where?"

A third militiaman, who had come up the road, replied: "They caught him wandering in an open field, sir. The blast must have stunned him."

"Can he talk?" the Captain asked.

"Yes sir, he won't stop. He keeps muttering something, and laughing. He says his name is Hamad."

"Bring him in for interrogation," said Captain Metzger, "and keep the women away from him. I want him in one piece." The Captain looked at the balding militiaman. "All right," he said quietly, "one minute. No more." He walked across the road to the Jeep with the radio, where he called for helicopters and mechanized patrols to converge on Jezzine, and a general alert of the West Bank towns. He did not look back at the roadside.

"Why did you want to murder a six-year-old kid, eh?" the balding Jew asked Faisal. Pressing his face close to him, he whispered fiercely, "Can you just tell me that? Why did you want to kill a six-year-old kid?"

Faisal said nothing. In his mind the chambers were closing in a labyrinth of echoes. The militiaman, weeping with helpless rage, shot him in the face.

Return

IN the dark hours before dawn on the morning of August 7, a bedside telephone awoke the commander of the Fourth Military District, Major General David Tamin, in his apartment in Jerusalem. He listened sleepily to his adjutant, then told him to put the officer in charge of the Beit Shal garrison, Captain Konrad Metzger, on the line. General Tamin sat up, listening to the Captain's cold, detailed report of the terrorist attack on the school bus. "This isn't war," the General growled, "it's murder!" He rang off, dressed, called for his adjutant, and drove through the quiet streets of Jerusalem to his staff headquarters. One hour later, on the urgent representation of General Tamin, an emergency meeting of the Israeli Cabinet convened in Tel Aviv. Justly outraged at the slaughter of the innocents of Beit Shal, it took the Cabinet only ten minutes to draft an order for the Israeli air force to launch a punitive strike. The details were left to General Tamin, and the ministers, finding themselves together at an early hour, took up the discussion of more important matters.

An exemplary reply was in order. On the theory of collective responsibility, General Tamin directed the reprisal not at any of the numerous guerrilla camps marked with red flags, but at the undefended Jordanian village of Marjouyan—this to convince the recalcitrant Arabs that they could not afford to pay the price which Israel was prepared to extract for continued guerrilla raids.

At sunrise of a hot, clear day, two Phantom F-4 fighter bombers lifted off the shimmering, mile-long runway of Luguna Air Base, carrying bombs with the destructive force equivalent to the broadside of a World War II battleship, to be dropped on the fragile houses and cobblestone lanes of Marjouyan. The Arab families awoke that morning to the sounds, once familiar in Warsaw, of dive bombing. Fifteen minutes later, having methodically razed half the village, the jets flicked a wing and turned for home. In the smoldering rubble, amid the cries of the wounded, fourteen men, eleven women, and twelve children lay dead or dying, while the bodies of five others, never found, were reported missing.

By the time the morning sun stood clear of the rooftops of Amman, justly outraged at the slaughter of the innocent citizens of Marjouyan, the Jordanian Army High Command, from a bombproof underground bunker outside the city, called down a thirty-minute artillery barrage on the Hebron Valley kibbutz of Tel Wasserman. The first shells came in when the families of the kibbutz were sitting down to breakfast. When the barrage lifted—the acrid smoke of the 120-mm-shell craters trailing across the morning fields on a gentle breeze—four Jewish men, two women, and six children were blown to pieces, and thirteen others lay wounded.

That afternoon the Associated Press wire reported that Israeli and Arab forces had exchanged fire across the Jordan River.

An hour after these events began, Salah, mud-spattered and dripping, pulled himself out of the river and with a last surge of strength walked up a ravine, where he threw himself down amid a rubble of stones. If the Jews cared to pursue him across the Jordan, he thought, they could kill him, and welcome to it. He would move no farther. All night he had been fleeing for his life through the darkness of Israel. And he had been alone.

As quickly as the explosion on the Jezzine road had told them that something had gone unexpectedly, hideously wrong, the Captain had started back down the slope. "The timers!" he shouted. "We've got to set them back!" He went along the transmission line, sliding in loose stone, changing the detonators to fire in five minutes. Salah hesitated above him at the last tower they had mined, remembering the Captain's own words, that if they fired the towers prematurely none of them would get over that hill alive.

Remembering that, Salah made his decision at once. He abandoned the Captain and started for the crest of the hill, struggling upward toward the edge of moonlight and the flashing radio beacon, trying to reach it before the plastic went off. He heard the Captain shout a final curse at him, but he was nearly over the top when the towers exploded. The concussion whined over the wires above him, and he threw himself on his face while the transmission lines collapsed in a storm of sparks. Unscathed, he stood up in an atmosphere of ozone and burnt insulation, and looked back for one final moment. He saw the machine guns opening up at them from the garrison, the patrols advancing. He heard the futile chatter of Ali's machine gun trying to hold them back. Deciding that if the Captain had chosen to die heroically he might as well die for something worth while, Salah ran over the moonlit slope of the hill, leaving Ali to hold off the patrols alone.

The flight down the rocky hillside had been a nightmare. As often as Salah fell he looked to the right, expecting to see the headlights of motorized patrols sweeping around the base of the hill to cut him off. But the mine had done its work; the road was cut. He reached the plain, stopped to think for a breathless moment, and struck boldly away from Jezzine, toward a ridge of rugged hills to the southwest.

Whatever the merit of his tactic had been, it had worked. Whether by inspiration or blind luck, he had chosen the most unlikely route out of Israel, the only one which the Jewish patrols, fanning out from Beit Shal, thought they could ignore. He was across the plain when the mine detonated the bridge. The helicopters, dropping flares in Jezzine, swung back at once toward the plain, confused. "Sweet, blessed little Arab bridge," Salah thought, and plunged down into the first dark ravines of the Jordan hills.

All night flares were dropped a mile or two on both sides of him; helicopters fluttered overhead on their way to new positions. Salah threw away his Sten and ammunition belt. He did not intend to fight. If he ran afoul of a Jewish patrol he wanted to be captured, not killed. If he were spotted he would throw up his hands and cry for

mercy. Why not? Of course, they might shoot him anyway, but if he kept the gun they were *sure* to shoot him.
What good had it done Ali to have died fighting? Was he
any less dead? Salah wondered, without the least irony,
how anyone could think that the life of another man, or
even a dozen men, was worth his own. Hero was a word
they put on a fool's death.

Salah ran over volcanic, barren hills, stumbled through
a maze of ravines, slid on his behind down the crumbling
sides of dry washes, dragged himself over sand dunes. At
dawn he was a mile from the Jordan River at a point (so
Salah guessed, staring at the opposite shore) several miles
south of Mokhtara. In five hours he had covered twenty-
five miles over terrain which no machine, and no animal
less stubborn and less frightened than man, could have
driven itself. He had climbed over klinkered ridges, hob-
bling on his injured leg. One impossible obstacle followed another. His ankle, twisted going in, was swollen
to the size of a melon. He was covered with welts and
cuts from sharp stones, his clothing was ripped; each time
he fell he lay face down and wept, then drove himself to
his feet, cursing with pain, to limp on, only to fall into
the stony embrace of the earth within another hundred
yards. All night a whine had filled his ears, the sound of
his own tortured breathing, as sharp as that of a suffocating animal. When at last he stole down to the edge of the
river in the morning light, he waited for half an hour in
the cover of the reed banks before he summoned enough
courage to splash across in a final, desperate lunge. At
every step in the water he had expected the burst of gunfire to hit his back. How badly he wanted to live! Then,
when he dragged himself out of the water and staggered
up the ravine, once more safely in Arab territory, he

found that it hardly mattered.

Turning over painfully, Salah now surveyed the far shore of the river. There was no sign of the enemy. He heard the distant, rolling thunder of an artillery barrage. No doubt the Jew was busy with his morning's work elsewhere. Pulling himself to his feet, he accepted the glum fact that he was the sole survivor. That mine! What the devil had it been? And Faisal—had he been on the hill with them, fighting beside the Captain during those last desperate minutes, or down on the road? Salah grunted with grim satisfaction, peered once more suspiciously at the Israeli side of the river, and limped away.

But that Captain Ali, he thought, almost smiling, there was a man, a true Arab soldier, staying behind like that to die fighting! So what if he had cursed him? Salah admired him nonetheless. The living could be generous. He looked up at the blue sky. The laugh that had been welling up within him broke irrepressibly forth. Ha, ha! But what fools men were, after all! And himself? No, perhaps they would never call him a Saladhine, but at least he was alive!

When he came to a road he began to walk north. For him, the end of the raid was as simple as that. He flagged down a produce truck, and told the driver to take him to El Husn. At first the driver, a fat little Jordanian on his way to the market in Amman, refused to believe that he was a Fatah. Where was his gun? Salah instead showed him his knife. "Okay! Okay! Take it easy!" cried the fat little Jordanian. "What's it to me?" By the time the truck rattled over the corrugated bridge into the camp, Salah had fallen asleep. He awoke with a start to find himself being lifted out as if he were dead. "Hands off!" he said. "Can't you see the shape I'm in? Treat these bones gently." A crowd quickly gathered, asking questions about the raid. Where was *Al Sakhr?* Where was the Captain? Had they given the Jews a fight? Salah assumed an ironic, indulgent air. "It was all a great success." Then, with a sly wink. "Everything went to hell!" Unable to walk, he was helped into a Jeep and driven up the hill to the command post, where he found the Major waiting for him, sitting at his accustomed place behind the field table, flanked by a dozen fighters.

The stucco room was foul with the odors of human sweat, tobacco, and kerosene, but to Salah the smells were sweet. Everyone but Kassim was listening avidly to the radio reports of the action that had begun at dawn. Blow and counterblow were being exchanged between artillery batteries on both sides of the Jordan. The positions at Shitar el Eid had been hit by counter battery fire. Units deeper in the Amman desert were sending shells over into the Jewish artillery. In retaliation for the deaths at Tel Wasserman, the Israeli air force had bombed the camps at Damour, Zahle, and Hambdoun. If they continued to escalate like this, mainline regiments would soon come into action. To Kassim, of course, it was all beside the point, these daylight bombardments. Let the armies fight. Sitting between Robert Shoemaker and the radioman, he was wrapped in his own thoughts, already contemplating the night's reprisals.

When he saw Salah enter he stood up. "Bring him a chair!" he ordered. "Can't you see that he is suffering? Zooheir, go down and bring Dr. Rashid at once."

Easing himself into the canvas chair, Salah extended his swollen leg. "It's nothing," he said, in mockery of what the younger fighters watching him—Jamal, Faoud, Rajah—expected to hear. He knew that he looked near death, with his torn clothing, scarred face and hands, exhausted, pale eyes enlarged by the remnants of his face grease. Heroically, with secret pleasure, he added, "I am just a little tired."

"Bring the doctor nevertheless," said Kassim. He regarded Salah with approval. "We of the people's army take care of our wounded." Zooheir dashed urgently out of the room, as if it were a matter of life and death.

Salah and Kassim, understanding one another, smiled. "Would you like a cigarette?"

Salah leaned forward with difficulty. "Thank you, Major." Kassim lit it for him, and he sat back, inhaled deeply, with real pleasure, and allowed the smoke to pass through his nose. Salah wondered for a moment if he hated Kassim; he decided that he did not. Then he felt suddenly alarmed and weak. The taste of the tobacco had made him sick. He did not have the strength left to hate anybody.

Briefly he made his report. The electrical station? No, impossible to hit. A mine field. The garrison right on top of it. Again he tried to despise Kassim. He watched him for some sign that he had known about that mine field, had, in fact, sent them to their deaths. But he saw only the bland, inoffensive face, the patient eyes. No, Salah thought, he was no match for Kassim. The rest of the questions he answered mechanically, dreaming of a bath, some cold food, and his cot, the sweet oblivion of sleep, of letting everything go, to awaken at twilight knowing only that he had survived. Salah wanted to laugh. Yes, he had survived! Only he! What did he care about Kassim?

"The towers?" Major Kassim asked.

Destroyed, along with a bridge and the road. Ali, Faisal, and Hamad? As far as he knew, dead. All dead.

A stunned murmur passed around the young men in the room. *Al Sakhr* dead! It was hard to believe.

Jamal interrupted the debriefing. "How did the Captain die?"

"He stayed on the hill to cover our retreat," Salah said. "The others died on the road. Ali was very brave."

Kassim glanced at him, warning him not to say too much. Salah understood—heroes did not bear close inspection.

"But weren't they with you on the hill?" asked Jamal, speaking of "the hill" reverently, as if it were already legendary, mystical. The Hill of *Al Sakhr*. The place of heroes.

"They volunteered to mine the road, to block the Beit Shal garrison," Salah replied generously. "It went off while they were setting it."

Robert Shoemaker coughed. "Not quite," he said, dropping his lanky legs off a stool onto the concrete floor. "A school bus ran over the mine. Twenty children were killed."

Salah squinted at him. "What are you saying?"

"The wire service in Tel Aviv had it this morning. AP expects to run the story tomorrow with photographs. They say it was quite a mess. One of your people, unidentified, was shot on the road. The women stripped the body and hung it by the heels from a tree."

The Major was sardonic. "Will your wire service run a photograph of *that?*"

Robert Shoemaker allowed himself a smile. "I doubt it. Do you want to make a statement, Major?"

Kassim sighed wearily. "You may say that we of the people's liberation army demand that all prisoners of war be treated fairly."

"I meant about the school bus."

"Ah, well," said Kassim, "tragic, of course. No doubt the Jew will use it for propaganda."

"Was it a deliberate act of terrorism?"

Kassim was evasive. "Last month the Jew bombed a school in Cairo. Was that deliberate terrorism?" He tapped out another cigarette. "Sixty children died. To-day women and children have died at Marjouyan. The ratio of such deaths is minor. They do not affect the struggle."

"For the civilians who die," Robert Shoemaker commented dryly, "the ratio is one hundred percent."

"I will take you to Marjouyan," said the Major, "and when your wire service carries a photograph of that atrocity, I will make an appropriately sympathetic statement concerning the incident of the school bus."

"I'll file a story with Amman," Robert Shoemaker promised, "if there's anything there."

It was time to begin the morning's work. Kassim turned the journalist's words to account. "Is there anything there?" he asked dramatically, looking up at the young men who stood around them. "How many of you have friends or relatives at Marjouyan?" Before any could reply, he turned back to Robert Shoemaker, his look more saddened than angry. "Tell me," he asked rhetorically, "what terrorism do you prefer, Mr. American newspaperman, the *plastiques* of Al Fatah or the bombs of the Israeli air force? A canister of napalm, I assure you, makes no distinctions whatever. A man? A woman? A child?" Kassim raised his eyebrows. "A cat? To a white phosphorus bomb they are all the same. At least the Fatah discriminates. We say 'That one, that one, and that one, over there, are guilty,' and kill them; the rest we try to leave alone. The Jew does not trouble to select. He kills wholesale, from a distance, without so much as soiling his fingernails. And for that you call him civilized!" Kassim's eyes narrowed with pleasure. "But then, aerial terrorism is an American technique. You are our guest. We do not wish to embarrass you." He turned to gaze at the wall map of Palestine. Raising both clenched fists, he addressed the fighters. "When you are across the river tonight, I want you to remember the women and children of Marjouyan! I want you to remember Captain Ali!" he said, almost chanting his litany. "I want you to remember Faisal! They were trapped on a hilltop fifteen miles within the Promised Land. And what did they do? They fought, and died—as men must!" The young fighters were ready for this exhortation; they listened passionately, assenting to everything, their eyes ablaze with fervor. Like *Al Sakhr*, they would go forward, and die! Like Faisal, they would be fearless! Kassim, long accustomed to manipulating the volatile fervor of youth, that thoughtless, all but useless enthusiasm, subdued his tone at once. He banked the heat of this furnace, in order to conserve it for the proper moment. With his fingers crossed before his face he looked sternly up at Jamal, who would lead the raid that night against the fortified settlements of the Bikhazi. Jamal was young, no older than Faisal, and Kassim, observing the beardless face, the frank expression in his eyes, thought with a moment of detached pity that this one, of course, would never return alive. Only the cynics, the realists like Salah, knew how to get back. Would Jamal have the sense to abandon his comrades at the critical moment? When he had five seconds to think, would he think only of himself? Ah, it was lamentable. Kassim felt it, as a memory of all the youths he had watched go to their pointless deaths. But instantly Kassim rebelled against this infirmity of sentiment. It was nothing to him what became of Jamal. Only what Jamal's life might be sold for in the way of blown-up canals, dead Jews, and frightened towns, only this mattered. Something deep within Kassim, a habitual voice of caution, warned him that he was in danger of committing the common error of mankind; on the day when he allowed himself the luxury of pity he, the Liberator, would be finished. Deir al Quamar, Marjouyan, the countless, insignificant deaths of the people—what were these to him? They would all die, sooner or later, by disease, carelessness, or bombardment; the unluckiest would die of old age, sniveling, groveling for one more hour's breath. Pah! The wretchedness of men! Kassim was genuinely revolted. Death was inevitable, therefore contemptible. The essential thing was to die with meaning. Yes, there was his vocation, to give them meaning! To weld them to his higher purpose. He was accountable only to his own, secret gods, the demons of History, merciless, unsparing, implacable. To have lived was nothing, to die everything. Would Jamal understand this dignity with which he, Kassim, invested him? Never! Kassim acknowledged it inwardly—if they knew, how they would hate him! How they would turn away, as if from a leper! They would refuse to obey! It was their destiny to fight and die, his to suffer his perpetual exile from the society of men. And for this he got nothing. Kassim felt at once distant, aloof, and lonely. His composure restored, he regarded Jamal with a new, cold vision, as a pawn to be moved on the board, a piece of wood to be given the dignity of a man, and of history.

In order to use them, Kassim thought, looking up at

Jamal, it was necessary only to despise them.

"Do you know your target?" he asked.

The look of awareness in Jamal's handsome eyes deepened. "Perfectly, sir, inside and out. I have studied the maps for days."

"And you can do the job?"

"I am confident," Jamal replied seriously. He looked at Rajah and Faoud for support. "We won't let the Jew stop us. We are young. We'll have luck."

"Luck has nothing to do with it," Kassim said, jabbing the air with his pencil. "You will succeed because, unlike the Jew, you are unafraid of death, because you use your death as a weapon. That is why you will reach the Bikhazi. Can you carry enough plastic to accomplish what I want?"

"With three men we can carry sixty pounds," said Jamal.

"And will it break the canals?"

"It will."

"And their compound?"

Rajah stepped forward. "I am packing in a mortar, Major. We will have ten rounds of sixty mm. Faoud is a crack mortarman."

Jamal added with boyish enthusiasm, his hands on the table, "Faoud can lay a shell in a rain barrel at two hundred yards, first shot!"

Kassim wondered where Jamal had learned that. In a movie? Secretly he smiled. But he was satisfied. They were ready. Having boasted before one another, they could never retreat. It remained only to send them out into the lonely daylight of the camp, into that torment of waiting where men's nerves bent like steel in a furnace. Relaxing his hold on them, Kassim allowed their enthusiasm to build.

"Good," he said, rising to his feet, "good! We must not let the Jew rest for a minute! I warn you, he is arrogant! He despises you! He imagined that Marjouyan will stop us! What is our answer?"

"We will hit him!" Rajah shouted.

"And we will hit him again!" cried Faoud.

Kassim embraced them as men. "Splendid! We will never stop hitting him! We will never relent! And because the Jew does not want to die," he prophesied, his eyes aflame, "one day he will fall to his knees. Hamdullah!"

With an abrupt change of tone, his manner once again mild and conciliatory, Kassim took Robert Shoemaker's arm. Softly, he said:

"I will now take you to Marjouyan, my friend. As people do not seem to interest you today, we will see how many dead cats we can find."

When Kassim and the others left Dr. Rashid came in to treat Salah. He cut off the boot, ripped the trouser leg at the knee, washed and loosely dressed the swollen ankle. Rashid, himself a demolition expert, looked down at Salah. "You'll live." He inquired with professional interest, "A good night?"

"Oh, lovely," said Salah. "Lovely."

"We will help you up to your tent," Jamal offered.

"Under the shoulders," Rashid said.

With Jamal on one side, Rajah on the other, and Faoud coming behind, they started across the camp. In the blazing white sunlight Salah's spirits rose. "Oh, this is fine," he murmured, so grateful to be alive that he felt like weeping. "Isn't this just fine?" He laughed out loud, feeling giddy. They bumped him, and he relished the pain in his leg. "Careful, you mules! Do you want to kill me? That's better."

Faoud ran to the front to offer him a cigarette. Salah took it, inhaling deeply.

"Tell us about last night," Faoud asked. "Did you kill many Jews?"

"Oh, dozens," Salah grunted. Shocked, he realized that this might be true. The taste went out of his mouth, and he spat away the cigarette. So it had been a school bus down there on the Jezzine road? But that was too hideous to believe. You couldn't trust an American. What did the journalist know about it? The Jews always lied about the Fatah raids. Comforted, Salah felt his mercurial spirits rise again. The pain in his foot continued deliciously.

"Who mined the bridge?" asked Rajah.

"I did," said Salah.

"And the towers?"

"The Captain and I did that together."

Jamal shook his head in wonder. "What a man Captain Ali was! How I wish I could have gone with him last night!"

Salah looked into Jamal's face. He recognized the open, youthful expression, the innocence which valued ideals above life. Saddened, he thought that Jamal had only hours to live. "Where were you born?" he asked.

"In Gaza," replied Jamal.

"Ah, then you grew up in a refugee camp."

"Yes, around Amman."

"Your parents?"

"My mother is alive."

Salah shook his head angrily, weakly, trying to free himself from their helping arms. "Then why, in the name of Allah," he asked. "do you want to cross the Jordan tonight? Don't you know what it will be like?"

Jamal was surprised. "Why," he said, "we go for the people."

"The people . . . !"

"For justice."

Salah groaned. "Justice—oh, Lord!"

Jamal looked at him, frowning. "But don't you believe in justice?"

"Justice? Of course I believe in justice," Salah answered ironically. "Just take a look at me. . . . Can't you see?"

"Freedom to the people!" cried Rajah.

"Yes, yes," cried Faoud, "we will fight to avenge *Al Sakhr!*"

"The people will win," Jamal said, supporting Salah under the right shoulder. "After all," he added, glancing at him, "the Jews aren't invincible. They'll have to crack."

"Oh, no," said Salah, "they are not invincible. No need to worry about that! They're just flesh and blood, like us." He laughed wearily. It was no use trying to save Jamal. His mouth was parched and dry; he felt as if half the flesh had been torn from his bones. "No need to worry about that at all! Someone will crack, all right."

Faoud danced in front of him. "We aren't afraid."

"Of course not. Do you suppose *Al Sakhr* was afraid!"

A truck lumbered by on its way to Marjouyan, covering them with dust. Salah looked up at the infinite blue dome of the sky.

He laughed. "Not for a minute!"

"Tonight the Bikhazi," said Rajah, holding Salah under the left arm. "Next month, Jerusalem! This time next year, Haifa!"

Salah squinted at him. "Do you really believe that?"

"But don't you want to go home?" asked Jamal incredulously.

"Home? Oh, yes," said Salah, stricken with a sudden, deep longing, "how I'd love to go home!"

"Oh, yes," echoed Faoud, leaping ahead to throw open the flap of the tent, "we'll all go home! Praise Allah! Hurrah for *Al Sakhr!* We are going to win! Hurray for everything!"

When the boys had left him alone and retreated down through the solitude of the camp, Salah stretched out on his cot. He groaned and closed his eyes. Again, he felt like weeping, with frustration, fatigue, a sense of doom. Voices from far away came to him. He thought of Jamal, who reminded him so much of Faisal. But Faisal was dead.

Then he saw the camp at Wadi Sirhain, the desert, the blazing tin box of the schoolroom, like a coffin on an August day. The stony, gray earth, people like stones moving.

Briefly, he saw the blue harbor of Haifa, the orange trees along the curvature of the sea, the trees of his youth.

Did he want to go home? Oh, Lord, yes, how tired he felt! How he wanted to go home, if only he knew where home was.

Left to himself, Salah indulged in the last human freedom. He turned on his side and went to sleep.

Victor Kolpacoff

BORN in Chicago in 1938, Victor Kolpacoff grew up in California, where he worked as a house painter and a hotel clerk in addition to earning a degree in history from San Diego State College. During 1966 he taught English at Shouf National College in Lebanon, where he completed work on his first novel, *Prisoners of Quai Dong*. Mr. Kolpacoff now lives with his wife and daughter in Geneva, New York, and teaches at Hobart College.